SHE'S A *DRAGON*, THAT'S WHAT SUZETTE MONAHAN IS.

And—I suddenly remember Suzette being mean to Alfie last week.

Suzette Monahan is Alfie's worst enemy and best friend rolled into one pinchy-faced, curly-haired package. Well, it's more like Suzette is Alfie's friend one day and her enemy the next day, with no reason behind the change. I can't keep up with it. Alfie usually jabbers about Suzette and her other friends at dinner so much that I don't really pay any attention. It's kind of just noise to me.

She hasn't been talking about them lately, though.

"What did Suzette do now?" I ask, feeling uneasy.

"She told the other little girls to act like Alfie's not there," Mom says, scowling into the sink. "Like she's invisible."

"But Alfie's not invisible," I say. "Even when we wish she was."

OTHER BOOKS YOU MAY ENJOY

EllRay Jakes Is a Rock Star!	Sally Warner/Jamie Harper
EllRay Jakes Is NOT a Chicken!	Sally Warner/Jamie Harper
EllRay Jakes Walks the Plank!	Sally Warner/Jamie Harper
Friendship According to Humphrey	Betty G. Birney
George Brown, Class Clown: Super Burp	Nancy Krulik/ Aaron Blecha
George Brown, Class Clown: Trouble Magnet	Nancy Krulik/ Aaron Blecha
Horrible Harry and the Green Slime	Suzy Kline/ Frank Remkiewicz
Horrible Harry Bugs the Three Bears	Suzy Kline/ Frank Remkiewicz
Horrible Harry Goes Cuckoo	Suzy Kline/Amy Wummer
Only Emma	Sally Warner/Jamie Harper
Super Emma	Sally Warner/Jamie Harper
Surprises According to Humphrey	Betty G. Birney
The World According to Humphrey	Betty G. Birney

EllRay Jakes the Dragon Slayer!

BY **Sally Warner**

ILLUSTRATED BY

Brian Biggs

PUFFIN BOOKS

An Imprint of Penguin Group (USA) Inc.

PUFFIN BOOKS
An imprint of Penguin Young Readers Group
Published by the Penguin Group
Penguin Group (USA) Inc.
375 Hudson Street
New York, New York 10014, U.S.A.

USA / Canada / UK / Ireland / Australia / New Zealand / India / South Africa / China
Penguin Books Ltd, Registered Offices: 80 Strand, London WC2R 0RL, England

For more information about the Penguin Group visit www.penguin.com

Published simultaneously in the United States of America by Viking Children's Books
and Puffin Books, imprints of Penguin Young Readers Group, 2013

17 19 21 22 20 18

THE LIBRARY OF CONGRESS HAS CATALOGED THE VIKING EDITION AS FOLLOWS:
Warner, Sally, date—
EllRay Jakes the dragon slayer! / by Sally Warner; illustrated by Brian Biggs.
p. cm
Summary: A mischievous eight-year-old boy helps his sister with a bully problem,
while facing a bully of his own at school.
ISBN 978-0-670-78497-4 (hardcover)
[1. Behavior—Fiction. 2. Bullies—Fiction. 3. School—Fiction. 4. Family life—Fiction.
5. African Americans—Fiction.] I. Biggs, Brian, illustrator. II. Title.
PZ7.W24644Elm 2013
[Fic] —dc23 20120304406

Puffin Books ISBN 978-0-14-242358-5

Printed in the United States of America
Book design by Nancy Brennan

For my long-time editor, Tracy Gates,

with affection and gratitude—S.W.

For Peter and Charles—J.H.

CONTENTS

☼ 1 ☼

THAT HOPEFUL LOOK

"Are you paying any attention to me at all, EllRay Jakes?" Mom asks from the driver's seat of our car, a Toyota so old they don't even make them anymore. It's the middle of April, and we are waiting in a humming line of cars in front of my little sister's day care.

"Wait. Yeah," I say, pushing Pause on *Die, Creature, Die*, my favorite handheld video game. I am almost at Level Six. "What?"

"I was *saying*, go inside and sign Alfie out," Mom says. "And tell her to hurry, please. I'm afraid to turn the engine off. Darn car battery," she adds. I can see the scowl on her face in the rearview mirror. "I have to call the auto club when we get home," she says. "If we can make it home without having to be towed."

"Do I *have* to get Alfie?" I ask, matching Mom's scowl with one of my own. "I had a sore throat yesterday. And last time you sent me in there, the little kids made me judge a contest out on the playground. Remember?"

Picture a combination of preschool versions of a TV singing contest and a wrestling match and you'll be close. It was terrible. One kid bit his best friend.

I'm working that sore throat, by the way. It's the reason I didn't walk home from school. Now, of course, I wish I had.

"You have to," Mom tells me, inching our car forward as the line moves. "She's not standing by the front door, naturally. Not our Alfie. That would be too easy. She'll be out back with her friends."

And she **REVS** the engine a little, as if reminding it what it's supposed to do.

Kreative Learning and Playtime Day Care is very strict about letting its little kids leave. They either have to be waiting right next to the front door, so the frazzled teacher with the clipboard can check off their names and then watch them go straight out to their car, or you have to walk all the way in and find the right little kid yourself. And then you have to sign them out, but only if you're on the approved list. That means parking the car, though, not waiting in line at the curb. And today, my mom's afraid to turn off our car.

When I grow up, I want to be so rich that I can buy a new car every time I get close to needing a new battery. Car batteries are boring things to buy.

"EllRay. *Move*," Mom says, her voice growing sharp.

And my mom is usually a very quiet lady.

"Okay, okay," I say, turning off my game and sliding it under my backpack so no bad guy can leap into the car and steal it when I'm gone.

It's my favorite thing!

"And make sure Alfie doesn't forget her new pink jacket," Mom tells me.

"She hasn't taken it off in three days," I remind her as I wrestle myself out of my seat belt. "I don't see how she could forget it."

And into Kreative Learning and Day Care I go.

★ ★ ★

I can't see Alfie anywhere in the main playroom—*naturally*, like my mom said. So I head out back. The whole rear play area is more like a giant cage with a fence around it than it is a playground, only there are so many fun things to do there that the kids don't notice.

I was hoping my sister would be in the covered patio where the battered playhouse and most of the girls are, but oh, no. And Alfie isn't on the slide or the swings, either. Those are pretty much being swarmed by leftover day care boys, including the kid who bit his friend that other time. A second teacher is trying to keep the boys from clogging up the slide. "One at a time!" she keeps calling out.

There's a job I never want to have.

"Alfie!" I call out, but she doesn't answer.

I search the playground with my **LASER-BEAM EYES**, the ones I use to score so high in *Die, Creature, Die*. And there she is with three other girls, over in the far corner of the yard, *of course*, by the tree, the bush, and the rabbit hutch. Alfie's golden-brown face has a funny expression on it.

I start to yell for her again, so I won't have to walk all the way over there to get her, but then I stop to watch, because I can't figure out what's going on. At first, it looks like all four girls are playing together. But then I see that it's really *three* girls who are together, with Alfie on the side, near the hutch. It reminds me of when my mom says, "Dressing on the side, please," when she's ordering salad in a restaurant.

The tallest of the three clumped-together girls is Suzette Monahan, who is a real pain, in my opinion, even though Alfie thinks she's so great. Suzette came over to our house one day, and my mom's still talking about it.

To say that Suzette is used to getting her own way is putting it mildly.

Today, Suzette has a long arm slung over each of the other two girls' necks. Alfie is turned away from them, staring down at the ground. Her shoulders are slumped. She's kicking at the dirt like that's the most interesting thing in the world to do, and some stuff goes flying through the air.

And I suddenly remember my old nursery school in San Diego, and the rabbit hutch we had there, and

Fuzz-Bunny, who was so kicky and grouchy that no one could even go near him. Hutches use heavy screens instead of regular hard floors on the bottom, so the rabbit poop—little pellets—just drops down onto the ground, where it's easy for teachers to rake it up. Rabbits' tidy poop is probably the only reason they are such popular day-care pets.

You're not supposed to *play* with the pellets, though. Or even kick them around.

And Alfie is usually so easily grossed-out. What's the deal?

One of the girls who has Suzette's arm hooked around her neck has a fluffy halo of brown hair. She reaches out toward Alfie, and she starts to say something. Alfie turns around. I know that hopeful look on her face, too—like it's been raining all Saturday, but the sun just came out.

But then Suzette yanks away the reaching-out girl, and she whirls both girls around like the three of them are on some lame carnival ride.

And Alfie is left just standing there.

Her smile goes behind a cloud. Even her new pink jacket looks sad.

"Rabbit poop girl," Suzette cries, tossing the

mean words over her shoulder like a *Die, Creature, Die* grenade. “Stupid pink jacket,” she shouts, piling on the insults. “Poop jacket!” she adds. Then she starts to haul her two captives away.

And these are Alfie’s *friends*?

“Hey, Alfie,” I call out as loud as I can, making sure the other girls can hear me. “Mom’s waiting out front for us. And we’re gonna do something really, really fun! With ice cream at the end of it! After we go shopping for dolls!” I add, inspired.

There. That ought to get ’em.

“EllWay!” Alfie shouts. And she starts running across the playground like she’s never been so happy to see anyone in her whole life.

We're only talking four years so far, but still.

I am going to have some explaining to do about fun, ice cream, and dolls once Alfie and I are buckled into our sputtering car. But it'll be worth it, seeing the look that's pasted on Suzette Monahan's mean little face right now.

She's jealous! *Good.*

But what is going on here at Kreative Learning and Playtime Day Care?

Probably nothing, I tell myself as Alfie throws her arms around me, giving me a surprisingly strong hug. Most likely, it was just some stupid game they were playing.

They were just having *fun.* Weird girl-fun, but fun. Weren't they?

And I put the whole thing in another part of my mind as I sign out Alfie and we head for the car.

Level Six, here I come!

2

TACO NIGHT

"What's up with Alfie?" I ask my mom a week later, after a perfect dinner of tacos, tacos, and more tacos. This happened because tonight was Taco Night, a popular new tradition on Wednesdays in my family. And then we had applesauce. It is my turn to help with the dishes, but instead of Alfie sticking around and pestering Mom and me, like she usually does, she has slumped off to her bedroom like a sad little comma with a dark cloud over its head.

My third grade teacher Ms. Sanchez said today that commas are our friends, because they break up long sentences and make them easier to understand. But I'm a short sentence guy.

I'm eight years old, and we live in Oak Glen, California. I go to Oak Glen Primary School, and as you already know, Alfie goes to Kreative Learning and Playtime Day Care, "*featuring computer skills and potty training*," my dad always likes to read from the big sign out front. He has almost stopped complaining about how they spelled "creative" wrong, because what's the point?

They must think it's cute, Mom says.

Alfie goes to day care because Dad teaches about rocks in a San Diego college all day, and my mom writes fantasy books for grown-up ladies.

That fantasy book thing is why Alfie and I have such unusual—okay, **WEIRD**—names, by the way. "Alfie" is short for "Alfleta," which means "beautiful elf" in some ancient language hardly anyone speaks anymore. And I'll tell you about my name some other time. Maybe.

"Alfie's got the blues, I guess," my mom tells me, running the water as hot as it will go as I scrape our dirty plates into the trash. There isn't much garbage to scrape on taco night, I have noticed. Not as much as two nights ago, when we had eggplant lasagna, which is just *wrong*. Eggplants should not pretend to be meat.

By the way, Mom rinses all our dishes sparkling

clean before she puts them in the dishwasher, which my dad says is "just like her." But who else would she be like?

"What does Alfie have to be sad about?" I ask, handing my mom a couple of scraped plates. "She's four. She doesn't even have homework. Her life is perfect."

"And you're the expert on other people's lives," Mom announces with a laugh, like she's narrating a TV show.

"What's her problem, then?" I ask. "Why is she so sad? Did a new Barbie come out a minute ago and she doesn't have it yet?"

"No," Mom says, scrubbing hard at an invisible spot on a dinner plate. "I think it's Suzette Monahan again, that little dickens."

A "little dickens" is not a good thing to be. Not the way Mom says it.

And—I suddenly remember Suzette being mean to Alfie last week.

Suzette Monahan is Alfie's worst enemy and best friend rolled into one pinchy-faced, curly-haired package. Well, it's more like Suzette is Alfie's friend one day and her enemy the next day, with no reason behind the change. I can't keep up with it. Alfie usually jabbers about Suzette and her other friends at dinner so much that I don't really pay any attention. It's kind of just noise to me.

She hasn't been talking about them lately, though.

"What did Suzette do now?" I ask, feeling uneasy.

"She told the other little girls to act like Alfie's not there," Mom says, scowling into the sink. "Like she's invisible."

"But Alfie's not invisible," I say. "Even when we wish she was. That's just dumb."

"Well, *you* know that, and *I* know that," my mom says. "But I think the other little girls are scared of Suzette, so they go along with whatever she says. And Alfie sure couldn't do anything to change their minds today."

"You should tell one of the teachers on Suzette," I say, thinking of some of the other bad things she's done—not even counting what I saw her do last week.

She's a **DRAGON**, that's what Suzette Monahan

is. A small, brown-haired dragon with mean green eyes.

Once she came over to our house for a play date, and when it was snack time, she demanded McDonald's. She didn't get it, but she demanded it.

And that very same time, she and Alfie snuck into my room to snoop around, which Alfie would never dare to do on her own. And Suzette messed up my bookcase and put a tutu on one of my soldier action figures.

And another time, before the rabbit poop day, Suzette threw torn-up paper in Alfie's hair at Kreative Learning, and Alfie didn't know it for like half an hour. And some girls laughed at her, and Alfie cried when she got home, because she thought they were making fun of her hair.

And a few weeks ago, Suzette said Alfie couldn't be the cutest girl in day care anymore, because *she* wanted to be the cutest from now on.

I don't know what the teachers are doing at that day care, besides guarding the front door and the slide. At Oak Glen, my teacher Ms. Sanchez might miss a few things here and there, but not big things like that. Not dragon things.

Suzette even scratched Alfie once with her claws, to make her let go of a puzzle piece! I'm the only one Alfie told about that.

Mom sighs as she wipes her hands dry. "It's usually better if kids can work out these things on their own," she informs me. "Unless there's some major bullying going on, I mean."

"What do you call this?" I ask. I can feel my face getting hot and my hands getting clenchy, which is a sure sign that I'm really mad.

See, I have to get mad *for* Alfie sometimes, because for some reason she doesn't know how to get mad on her own. Except at *me*, when I won't play dolls with her, which I have decided will be always.

Sometimes I even get mad at Alfie for not getting mad.

"It's not quite bullying yet," Mom says, like she knows this for a fact.

Of course, I have a little more information than she does. "Well, tell me when you think it *is* bullying," I tell her. "Because then I'm gonna kick me some Suzette Monahan—"

"EllRay Jakes!"

"Bootie," I finish, laughing.

By now, Mom is laughing too. "But you would never kick a girl," she reminds me, not that I need any reminding.

"I know," I say. But I narrow my eyes to look jokey-mean.

“Why don’t you go talk to your little sister right now?” Mom says, her voice getting soft. “I think she could use some cheering up, don’t you?”

“I guess,” I say, hiding my sigh, because cheering up Alfie usually involves a whole lotta listening to a whole lotta Alfie-talk.

But sometimes, like my dad says, you just have to “man up.”

And this is probably one of those times.

✲ 3 ✲

OVER THERE

Alfie's bedroom door is open, but I pretend-knock anyway because I'm trying to train my little sister to knock before she barges into *my* room. Fat chance. "**KNOCK, KNOCK,**" I call out.

Alfie's room is an explosion of pink and purple, her two favorite colors. I'm not against a person having favorite colors, even if they're not sports team colors. But that doesn't mean you have to decorate your whole life with them. That's what Mom did, though, repainting Alfie's baby room when she turned four. And Alfie's got silver stars on her ceiling now, too.

I wouldn't mind a few of those silver stars on *my* ceiling.

Alfie is sitting cross-legged next to a tangled heap of dolls in front of the long mirror on her closet door. She's watching herself play with one of the dolls. Alfie waves a pale, skinny doll arm in the air like it's saying "Hi."

"Come in, EllWay," she tells me, not sounding very happy to see me. She can't say my name right, but I know who she means. She goes back to watching herself play in the mirror.

"Watcha doin'?" I ask, collapsing next to her onto the shaggy rug. I can see Alfie's new pink jacket stuffed way back under her bed. "Didn't you like your tacos?"

"They were okay," Alfie says, shrugging.

Alfie just puts cheese in her tacos. No meat, just cheese. But that's her decision, and you should get to choose how boring you want to be in life.

"Look," Alfie says, staring into the mirror as she waves her doll's arm again. "It's almost the same over there."

"*Over there*" means in the mirror, I guess.

"It's *exactly* the same," I say. "Only it's opposite, because you're seeing a reflection in a mirror."

"That's not true. It's not the same," Alfie says, scowling. "Because this is my left hand, right?" she asks, holding her left hand up in the air. “Mom put a red rubber band around my wrist once, so I’d always memember.”

That’s Alfie-speak for “remember.”

“Right. I mean, *correct*,” I tell her, so we don’t get mixed up.

“But over there, for the mirror girl, it’s her right hand,” Alfie says.

“Correct. It’s opposite,” I chime in, only now I’m trying to sound more sure of myself than I’m feeling. Because—how could left suddenly turn into right like that? “And the mirror girl is you, by the way,” I add.

“But that’s not the only thing that’s different,” Alfie informs me, ignoring what I just said about the mirror girl. “Sometimes things move a little over there, or they change, and you can barely notice. You have to look real hard.”

“Huh?”

“In the mirror,” Alfie explains, her voice patient.

“No. Things don’t change,” I tell her. “Everything there is exactly the same as here, in real life.”

“Nuh-uh. It’s better,” Alfie says, still staring at

herself in the mirror. “Because no one’s invisible over there.”

“Nobody’s invisible *here*,” I say, wishing again that I could kick Suzette Monahan—in the shins or something, only kicking is girly. And like I said before, boys don’t kick or hit girls. Not in my family. It’s wrong, and my dad would freak. He has very old-fashioned—and strict—manners. He likes everyone to behave.

If Dad knew Alfie was being picked on at day care, for example, he would go nuts. And then he'd start an official Oak Glen committee to investigate the matter. I'm sure my mom hasn't told him yet. I'm positive.

"They're invisible at day care, though," Alfie says, not backing down. "*I'm* invisible at day care. Suzette says so." She looks down at her golden brown arm like she's making sure it's still attached to the rest of her.

"Suzette Monahan's not the boss of the world," I tell Alfie. "You should tell those other girls she's just *wrong*. Who else is your friend over at Kreative Learning?" I think my friend Corey's little sister goes there, and Jared's brother does, too.

"Mona is my friend, kind of," Alfie says, giving her arm a couple of experimental pokes. "And Arletty. But Suzette is my *best* friend there."

Mona and Arletty are probably those other two girls I saw that day. "Why do you keep saying Suzette's a friend?" I ask. "She's mean to you."

"I wish Suzette would start picking on someone else," Alfie says, ignoring my question. "Then we could *all* start picking on someone else."

"No! That's a terrible idea," I tell her. "Why do you guys have to pick on *anyone*? I mean, how would Suzette like it if kids started picking on her?"

I wish they would! Just to teach her a lesson about leaving Alfie alone!

"Mona and Arletty would never do that, EllWay," Alfie tells me, her eyes wide in the mirror as she meets my gaze. "They're nice. Anyway, bullying's not allowed at day care. There's a poster next to the sink and everything."

"What do you think *this* is?" I ask, trying not to shout. "Saying you're invisible?"

"She's not hitting me," Alfie points out. "Or even calling me names. She's just teasing me sometimes. And saying I'm not there." She pokes herself again.

"You should tell her to stop," I say. "Or I will. Want me to call her?"

What am I *saying*? How did I suddenly get so involved in this mess?

"What would you say?" Alfie asks, curious.

"That it's mean for her to treat you like that. Or *you* could tell her," I say, sounding eager, because it would be better coming from Alfie, wouldn't it?

What does Suzette Monahan care what I think?

Anyway, Alfie should be the one who's mad at Suzette, not me. Why doesn't Alfie have the same getting-mad ingredient in her that I do? What's *wrong* with her?

"I guess I could ask Suzette to make it stop," Alfie says, like the idea just **POPPED** into her brain with no help from me. But whatever.

"Good idea. Why don't you do it?" I say. "Tomorrow?"

"What day is tomorrow?" Alfie asks, picking up another doll and waggling it really close to the mirror, watching carefully for any random changes "over there," I guess.

"Thursday," I tell her, thinking about the now-banished pink jacket.

"Hmm," Alfie says, like she's really thinking. "Maybe I'll do it Fwiday."

Which is Alfie-speak for "Friday."

"Promise?" I ask.

"I promise I *might*," she says.

"You should at least hang up your new jacket," I tell her.

"Maybe I don't like it anymore," she says, not looking at me.

"Huh," I say. And that's about as good as it's gonna get, I tell myself, jumping to my feet and making a quick escape from Alfie's extremely frilly, pink and purple room.

That's enough Alfie Jakes for one night.

4

BUSY BEES

"Stop buzzing, all you busy bees," Ms. Sanchez calls out to get our attention. It is now the next day, a cold Thursday morning, and pretty soon we will go outside for nutrition break. My nutrition will be raisins and little square cheese crackers, but mostly I just want to run around with my two best friends at Oak Glen Primary School, Corey Robinson and Kevin McKinley. My legs are already itching, and I just sat down!

"***BZZ, BZZ,***" Kry Rodriguez says with a big smile on her face as she settles back into her seat.

Nobody ever gets mad at Kry, not even Ms. Sanchez, who is the prettiest teacher at Oak Glen. I can prove that, because the kids in my class voted once. Kry is the nicest person in our class. She came in late, way after September. Maybe that's why she has never been in the middle of any of our battles.

Kry's shiny black bangs go almost all the way down to her big brown eyes.

"No last-minute buzzing," Ms. Sanchez says, still sounding playful, but about at the *end* of playful, if you know what I mean. "We have work to do. Language Arts, to be precise."

Ms. Sanchez is always precise. That means exact, with no messing around.

"Settle," she says in a different voice, and we do, because you can't push it with Ms. Sanchez. If you really goof up, which Jared Matthews did just once, the whole class has to copy out an article from *Fascinating Facts for Young People.* Word for word. And those facts aren't all that fascinating, believe me.

So even Jared settles down, because he doesn't want everyone to be mad at him again.

Next to me, Annie Pat Masterson lines up two sharp pencils, in case pencil number one breaks, I guess. But she's okay. She likes fish—*alive* ones—and has bouncy red hair. Her best friend is Emma McGraw, the second-littlest kid in Ms. Sanchez's class.

Guess who is number one? Me. EllRay Jakes. But I'm gonna start growing pretty soon, and then watch out! I might even be a Laker some day. The tallest one.

"We will be writing a personal narrative today," Ms. Sanchez says. "That means you will tell a story in writing, but in an organized way."

She says "in an organized way" as if she doesn't really think it will come true, but she has her hopes—like when Mom tells Alfie, "You'll finish those peas and you'll like them, young lady."

"We'll start with a helpful worksheet so you can stay on track," Ms. Sanchez says, looking for someone to help her pass stuff around. Two hands shoot up into the air: Cynthia Harbison and her friend Heather Patton, who says she's allergic to coconut.

Cynthia is the bossiest—and cleanest—girl in our class.

"Okay, Cynthia," Ms. Sanchez says with a very small sigh, and she hands Cynthia the papers. Cynthia passes them around like she's handing out parking tickets.

I look at the paper. It has five questions on it.

1. What happened?
2. When did it happen?
3. Where did it happen?
4. Can you give us some details about it?
5. How did it end?

She left out "*Why did it happen?*" which I think can be the most interesting part of anything, even if sometimes you don't *know* why something happened. For instance, I don't know why that mean dragon Suzette Monahan is picking on Alfie. But it's happening anyway.

"Are you listening, EllRay?" Ms. Sanchez is asking, which means—I guess—that she's been saying something.

"**DOINK! DOINK! DOINK!**" Stanley says under his breath, and Jared smirks.

"Uh, sorry. No," I say, because I have learned the hard way that it's better to tell the truth when this happens, or else your teacher might ask you to explain things again to the whole class, since you've been listening so well. And then what?

"I was telling the class that I want you to

think of something that happened in your life recently," Ms. Sanchez says. "Not a huge event, just a small one. And then use this worksheet to write about it. And use your friend the comma correctly, please."

Heather's hand shoots up into the air once more. I think she was born that way. "Can I put unicorns in mine?" she asks. "Real ones, not stuffed animals?"

Okay, now that's just goofy, because—*real unicorns*?

"*Bogus*," Jared Matthews cough-says into his big freckled hand. Jared is the boy version of Cynthia in my class, meaning he's bossy. Not that he's like a girl.

Ms. Sanchez taps her foot. She always wears fancy shoes. My mom says she doesn't know how Ms. Sanchez can stand in them all day, especially the ones with pointy toes, but the girls in my class love them. I've actually heard them talk about it. Which is also goofy.

Ms. Sanchez clears her throat. "If you've had a recent, real-life experience involving a living, breathing unicorn, Heather, and you can use your commas correctly, I'm sure we'd all like to hear about it. So pick up your pencils, ladies and gentlemen," she says to us all, "and please begin."

And even though our stomachs are growling with starvation, we do.

* 5 *

MY PERSONAL NARRATIVE

Writing this wasn't as easy as I thought it would be, and I was the last one finished, but there was only one real-life thing I could think to write about for my personal narrative. My spelling, punctuation, and even my words were a little worse than what you are about to read, but here goes. My personal narrative is called "Alfie's Problem."

1. WHAT HAPPENED?

My mom said my sister Alfie was sad.

Five minutes later, Alfie told me her best friend at day care was mean to her. So that is Alfie's problem.

2. WHEN DID IT HAPPEN?

My mom told me Alfie was sad when we were washing the dishes.

Alfie told me about her problem five minutes after

that. This happened last night. If you wanted to know when was the girl mean, it was yesterday. But I also know she was mean to Alfie longer ago than that.

3. WHERE DID IT HAPPEN?

My mom told me about Alfie being sad in the kitchen. That is where we wash the dishes in my house.

Alfie told me about her problem in her bedroom, when we were sitting on the rug.

If you are asking where was the girl mean, it was at day care, like I said before. It is called Kreative Learning and Playtime Day Care. (Please do not mark me down for spelling "creative" wrong. That is how they spell it over there. My dad already complained.)

4. CAN YOU GIVE US SOME DETAILS ABOUT IT?

Yes! Our kitchen is mostly white. My mom washes the dishes before she even puts them in the dishwasher. That is just like her, my dad says.

Alfie's bedroom is purple and pink and has lots of dolls in it. Alfie was playing with one of them the whole time. The rug is pink.

If you want details about why was Alfie sad, the girl who was mean is named Suzette Monahan. She messed up my room once. Alfie likes her and thinks she is a friend, but she is not. One time she threw paper in Alfie's hair, and Alfie didn't know it, and some kids made fun of her.

Yesterday, Suzette told the other girls in day care to act like Alfie was invisible, and they did. That made Alfie very sad.

5. HOW DID IT END?

It ended when I left Alfie's room and went into my own room to play *Die, Creature, Die*. It is my favorite game! I am already at Level Six!!

If you mean how did the problem end, it didn't. It is still going on. I told Alfie that she should tell Suzette to quit it, because how would Suzette like it if someone did that to her? Alfie said maybe she would tell her on Friday. That means tomorrow, but I do not know if she will do it or not. Alfie is only four years old. She is not very organized yet, or very brave.

The End.

"Very nice, EllRay!" Ms. Sanchez wrote at the bottom when she handed the worksheet back just before lunch. "I'm sorry Alfie is having this problem. When you correct your narrative, however, please make it more *your* story, and tell us what it's like being Alfie's big brother. Okay?"

And of course I'm not about to say, "No, it's *not* okay!" am I?

Because Ms. Sanchez is the teacher, and I'm just a kid.

And—we're working on it *again*? We already did it once!

I wish I'd kept my big mouth shut—even though I didn't say a word.

But you know what I mean.

✲ 6 ✲

MR. NOBODY

"Dude," my friend Kevin says when finally, after about a hundred hours, Ms. Sanchez lets us loose for lunch. "What took you so long this morning? You missed part of nutrition break." It is still cold outside, and the wind is blowing. But at least it isn't raining yet.

Some kids have chosen to stay in the cafeteria for lunch, but not us, and not a few of the girls. You're not allowed to run around inside, and my legs want to run.

"Yeah," Corey chimes in as I reach into my bag for a sandwich. "You wrote a *ton*, EllRay."

"I was telling about my little sister," I say. "Why? What did you write about?"

"I wrote about spraining my ankle yesterday," Fiona McNulty calls out from the other lunch table, even though I wasn't asking her.

See, there is a boys' table in our lunch area at Oak Glen, and a girls' table. But they are pretty close together, and sometimes we can hear what the girls are saying.

"You're always spraining your stupid ankle," Stanley Washington says, after chomping down on a big sandwich in a hamburger bun that makes my mouth water just to look at it, even though Stanley and I are not exactly friends lately. You can see pieces of sandwich in his mouth as he talks, but even that doesn't shut the girls up.

"She is not," Cynthia says back. "Anyway, you know she has weak ankles. Poor little Fiona," she adds, patting Fiona's skinny back.

And Fiona smiles like anything. She holds out a pipe-cleaner ankle for evidence. It has a stretchy tan bandage around it, the kind that is always called "flesh-colored," only it's not. Not *my* flesh color, anyway. I'm brown, and so is Kevin, and two of the girls in our class who are friends from church. And so are a lot of people. Maybe not all that many in Oak Glen, California, but Oak Glen isn't the center of the universe.

Kevin clears his throat, which is a signal that

he's about to say something. "My personal narrative was about learning to swim really far last summer," he says.

"Huh. I can already swim far," Cynthia announces from the girls' table.

"I wasn't writing about *you*," Kevin points out. "I was writing about me. Anyway," he adds, "Corey can swim farther than everyone in our class put together. So, ha ha."

It's true about Corey. He is already a champion swimmer. He sometimes smells like chlorine from his early morning workouts. He has trophies and everything.

"I wrote about cleaning out my aquarium," Annie Pat says. She is the second-smallest *girl* in the third grade. Like I said before, Emma McGraw is the first-smallest girl. "I was so scared," she adds, shivering from either the wind or from being scared, who can tell? "Because one of my tropical fish jumped out of the little bowl I put it in while I was scrubbing the aquarium."

"Then maybe you shouldn't hold innocent animals captive," Cynthia says, her snooty nose high in the air. I guess she figures that she's so perfect, she can start in on correcting all of us, now.

And is a fish even an animal? I don't know, but Annie Pat gasps. She would never harm an animal *or* a fish. In fact, she wants to be a fish expert when she grows up. I forget the exact name of the job.

Emma, who is best friends with Annie Pat, is all over Cynthia in a second. "She's not 'holding them captive,' *Cynthia*," she says, her cheeks turning even pinker than they already were. "She's taking care of them. She's *protecting* them, and it's a lot of hard work."

"Yeah," Annie Pat says, having recovered from Cynthia's insult. "*Cynthia.*"

"What did you write about for your personal narrative, Cynthia?" Kry asks like she's really interested, brushing her shiny black bangs out of her eyes.

"I wrote about organizing my closet," Cynthia announces, chin still in the air.

Okay, now that's just sad. I mean, I'm not saying it didn't happen. And I'm not saying there weren't some details about it, or that it ended. But *writing* about it?

Everyone knows that all you have to do with

closets is to jam your stuff inside and then close the door real fast, before it can tumble back out.

Done!

Even some of the girls over at the girls' table are looking sideways at each other, hearing Cynthia's personal narrative topic.

"You should *see* her closet," Heather says, jumping to Cynthia's defense so fast that the long, skinny braid she usually wears on top of her hair swings across her face like a pendulum. "It's the best closet in the world!"

"*Now* it is," Cynthia says, shrugging modestly. "I even put a little chair in it when I was done, and my daddy built a special rack for all my headbands."

Cynthia wears a headband to school every single day. She scrapes her hair back like she's mad at it.

Her father makes the best sandwiches in the world, by the way. Me and my friends **DROOL** when we look at them, sometimes. That's what she should have written about. I didn't know Mr. Harbison could build stuff, too.

My college professor dad *hates* doing chores around the house. But he does like working in the garden. The rose bushes that looked like thorny

sticks in January have leaves on them now. He checks them every day. I'm not sure what he's looking for.

"*My* narrative was about the last time this little boy named Anthony came over," Emma says, starting to giggle. "He's only four, and he's really funny."

Cynthia sniffs, probably still thinking about her organized closet. "I met him once," she tells us.

"See, we were going to make some peanut butter cookies with fork marks on them," Emma explains. "Only he—"

"Too bad you don't have any real brothers or sisters," Heather interrupts. "Or you could have written about *them.*"

Emma is an only child, see, which I have to admit sometimes sounds pretty good to me. But Heather has this teenage sister she's always talking about. She must think that earns her special points or something—like she's an honorary teenager herself, just from living with one.

"Yeah. Too bad," Cynthia fake-sympathizes.

The girls have hijacked this lunch conversation big-time! They always do that.

"Being an only child wasn't what Emma was writing about," Annie Pat argues, sticking up for Emma even if Emma doesn't need her to.

"But who cares about a four-year-old kid?" Cynthia asks Emma—and me, I guess. Because I wrote about Alfie.

I care. I care about Alfie, anyway, since I don't know Emma's Anthony. I kind of have to care about Alfie, at least until she learns how to take care of herself.

Or until I teach her to.

A couple of the boys have ditched the shivering lunch crowd by now, even though the bell hasn't rung yet. Jared and Stanley are chasing each other around and around. It looks like fun. Why am I still sitting here?

I cram my trash into my lunch sack and stand up. Kevin does, too.

"Good riddance," Cynthia calls over from the girls' table.

"Who's she talking to?" Kevin asks, like he's really wondering.

"Mr. Nobody," I say back, laughing.

"And where does Mr. Nobody park his car?" Kevin asks, starting in on a dumb old joke of ours that still cracks us up.

"**IN THE MIRAGE!**" we both shout.

The girls are looking at us like we're nuts, but who cares?

We're gone!

7

STILL INVISIBLE?

"Are you still invisible?" I ask Alfie after dinner that night, when Mom and Dad are busy with something else. Paying bills, probably. Alfie and I are in my room, for a change, and Alfie is playing with one of my action figures that changes from a truck to a robot to a killer insect. She has been talking to it in baby talk, which is messed up.

"I'm only invisible at school, not here," Alfie says, letting the half-changed action figure droop a little. "Mona whispered something to me when we were playing at the dress-up box, but Suzette caught her. So after that, Mona beed quiet."

"But you're going to talk to Suzette tomorrow. Friday," I say like it's a fact.

Sometimes this works with Alfie, like when I say on a Friday night, "It's my turn to choose the cartoons tomorrow morning, remember?" Even though it isn't really my turn, it's hers. Only I don't feel like watching *Pink Princess Fairies* or *Itty Bitty Kitties*. Can you blame me?

"I might talk to her," Alfie says, shaking my action figure as if that is what makes it change. "Why doesn't this *do* anything?" she asks, frowning. "And don't you have any clothes for it? It has to stay *bare*?"

I don't even bother answering such a goofy question, because—clothes for a killer insect? Or for a robot or a truck, for that matter? What's it going to wear, pants and a hat?

"You have to talk to her," I say. "Look, we'll practice. Let's pretend you're you, okay? And I'm Suzette. What are you going to say to me? To Suzette?"

"But I thought you didn't like playing pretend," Alfie says, her brown eyes wide.

"I'll do it just this once," I tell her. "You have to learn, Alfie. And I guess I'm the one to teach you. Now, you be you, and I—"

"I'm *alweady* me," Alfie argues. "That's not pretending."

"But pretend you're talking to Suzette. *Go.*"

"*You* go," she mumbles.

"Okay," I reply, hiding my sigh. "Hi, Alfie," I say in a loud and whiny voice. "Why are you still hanging around? Can't you take a hint?"

"What's a hint?" Alfie asks me, EllRay, frowning again. "I forget."

"It's like a little clue," I try to explain. "Like if I said you are going to eat something crunchy for breakfast, and it comes in a box. Guess what it is?"

"Toast is crunchy," Alfie says, thinking about it.

"But it doesn't come in a box," I remind her.

"It could," Alfie points out. "If you put it there. Cereal wasn't *born* in a box."

"I'm Suzette Monahan," I say, trying hard to get back to the point. "And I'm saying, 'Get lost, Alfie Jakes. You are invisible to me and my friends.'"

"They're my friends, too," Alfie argues, finally getting into it. "And they're only minding you because you're so mean, Suzette. And you *scratch*."

"Who cares?" I say in my best Suzette voice. I pretend I am fluffing up my headful of brown curls like I think they're so great. As if they're what gives me my dragon powers. I'm glad my friends Corey and Kevin can't see me! "I'm the boss, and that's what matters," I continue, being Suzette.

"Those girls have to do what I say, *or else*."

"But they already did what you said," Alfie says, her voice wobbling a little. "Can't you boss them to do something else?"

"No," I say, shrugging in that I-don't-*think*-so way like Suzette did the time when my mom offered her homemade oatmeal cookies instead of saying okay, she would drive everyone to McDonald's. "I'm not bored yet. I'm having too much fun."

"But why is making me invisible *fun*?" Alfie says, tears filling her eyes. This makes them look even bigger than they already are, which is huge.

Pretending is harder than I thought. "Don't cry," I whisper.

"Are you Suzette now, or are you EllWay?" she whispers back, wiping her eyes.

"EllRay. But just for a minute. Now I'm Suzette again," I tell her, changing my voice. "It's fun because it bothers you so much," I say in my best stuck-up Suzette way. "Why *wouldn't* I do it? What else is there to do around here? You *care* the most. That's why it's fun."

"I could tell the teacher on you," Alfie says,

trying to put up a fight, if only a puny one.

"Go ahead," pretend-Suzette says. "Everyone will think you're a tattletale, and I'll say you're lying." Now *I'm* getting into it.

"Then I'll tell my mom," Alfie says, trying a different idea. "And she'll call your mom, and they'll talk. *Then* you'll be sorry."

"No, I won't. Go ahead and tell your mom. I don't care," I say with a Suzette sneer. "I can handle *my* mom. Anyway, she's too busy to care what bothers you."

"Then she's mean, too," Alfie says, slamming my action figure to the ground so hard that I almost forget for a second to be Suzette Monahan.

POOR TECHNO-ROBO-BUG!

Alfie's really angry, I can tell. Electric sparks are practically coming out of her soft, puffy black braids, she's so mad. But angry is better than droopy any day of the week, I remind myself.

"That's good, Alfie," I tell her.

"Be quiet, Suzette!" Alfie yells.

"No. I'm EllRay again," I say quickly, trying to calm her down before Mom and Dad come pounding up the stairs to see what's wrong. "Can't you pretend you don't care?" I suggest.

"I am a good pretender," she says, smiling. "It's one of the things I love best about me."

"Me too," I say, laughing. "So are you gonna say something to Suzette about not caring? Tomorrow morning? First thing? And get this whole disaster over with?"

"Maybe," Alfie says, cautious once more.

But I can tell that I've at least planted the idea in her head.

And best of all, she thinks it's *her* idea—which makes me a pretty good teacher, right? And a very good big brother?

You're welcome, Alfie!

8

IN FRONT OF THE WHOLE CLASS

"My shoes got wet on the way to school," my friend Corey complains the next morning. It is Friday, the third-worst day of the week for rain to happen. The first and second worst days are Saturday and Sunday, of course, because who wants to spend the weekend indoors?

Mr. Nobody, that's who. The guy who parks his car in the mirage.

"You're wet all the time anyway, Corey, 'cause you're alway in the pool, aren't you?" Kevin points out as we stash our backpacks in our cubbies, which they call "cubicles" in the third grade. Only really, they're the same as they were in kindergarten.

Just the word has changed.

There are probably lots of things that are like that.

"Sneakers are different," Corey says in his gloomiest voice. "You can't get 'em dry. I'm **SQUELCHING**."

Around us, the girls in our class are chattering like crazy. It's as if the April rain has revved them up in some weird way. "Ooh! Darling boots," Annie Pat is saying to Emma, who is holding out one of her legs for inspection.

They're lime green. The boots, I mean.

Girls have completely different clothes for when it rains. Most boys just put on another layer, and they always forget their umbrellas, if they even have umbrellas in the first place. Jared Matthews—who can be kind of bossy, remember?—is peeling off a damp brown sweater that looks like a layer of bark or lizard skin. His face is turning red, he's wrestling with that sweater so hard.

"Come on, everyone," Ms. Sanchez calls out from her desk, which is like Army headquarters for her. "We have lots of work this morning. It's personal narrative day!"

"We already did that," Cynthia Harbison tells her, raising her hand while she's already talking.

“We corrected them for homework last night,” she adds as she takes her seat, neat as can be. Have I mentioned how clean Cynthia is? It’s actually kind of creepy.

“Thank you, Miss Harbison. I realize that,” Ms. Sanchez says. “But today, we’ll read a few of them aloud. That’s an entirely different skill set.”

“We have to read in front of the whole class?” Corey cries out, unable to control himself. Corey hates doing *anything* in front of the class, even taking something up to Ms. Sanchez’s desk. Even though it’s not that big a class, and everybody likes him.

That’s weird, isn’t it, how scary it can be to have to stand up in front of people, even when you know them? I guess it’s because nobody wants all those eyeballs staring at them. Or maybe they’re afraid they’re going to make fools of themselves. I should say of *himself*, because some of the girls in my class are looking excited at the idea of reading their narratives aloud. A couple of girl-hands have already shot into the air.

“We’ll get started right after I take attendance,”

Ms. Sanchez says. "I'll decide who to call on then."

Not me, not me, not me, I think, squinching my eyes shut to help make my wish come true.

★ ★ ★

"You're up next, EllRay," Ms. Sanchez says as Cynthia takes her seat before nutrition break. "And Cynthia," she adds, "I'm sure we've all learned something valuable about organizing a closet. Also, thank you, Emma, for telling us the terrible tale of that forty-five-dollar library book about amphibians that you lost. You had us all shivering in our boots. Thank goodness you finally found it. And now, I present Mr. Jakes, who is going to tell us what it's like being a big brother. EllRay?"

Someone groans. Probably Stanley, and for no reason.

"But is there enough time?" I ask, like my narrative is so interesting and exciting that I don't want to cut it short because of mere nutrition break, or like I don't want everyone's stomach growling while I'm trying to read my personal narrative. My *private* personal narrative.

As if there's such a thing as privacy around here!

I would have written about almost stepping on a rattlesnake once in Arizona if I'd known we were going to have to read our narratives aloud!

I will never live down this wimpy, way-too-personal narrative.

"There's time," Ms. Sanchez says, nodding. So I plod to the front of the class and stand at the corner of her desk. "Nice and loud, EllRay," she reminds me. "No mumbling."

Mumbling is a big no-no with Ms. Sanchez. "Stand up, speak up, and look people in the eye," she always tells us.

"Okay," I say, and I clear my throat in a Kevin-like way. "Being a Big Brother, by EllRay Jakes," I begin.

"Louder, please," Ms. Sanchez tells me. "Speak to the very back row, EllRay."

"Okay," I say again, and I start reading.

★ ★ ★

When I have finished, I tuck my chin down and scurry back to my seat, hoping no one will have the chance to ask any questions or give me advice about how to be an even better big brother. Some girls in my class have a lot of advice to give, I have noticed.

But it turns out I don't have to worry about that—inside the classroom, anyway—because it's finally, finally time for nutrition break.

And I have earned my snack today, believe me.

9

EXTREME DODGEBALL

"We can go outside. It stopped raining," Jared Matthews announces, sounding proud, like he personally changed the weather for us. He is pawing around in his lunch bag for his snack, which will be a large one. Like I said, Jared is the biggest kid in our class.

The whole cubicle room smells weird, like a mixture of food, floor cleaner, and wet jackets, but everyone is still hungry.

"And Jared and me, we're in charge of the kickballs," his friend Stanley says, his glasses gleaming. He is wearing *two* plaid shirts today—layers, see?—even though Cynthia once said the shirts he wears makes him look like a walking picnic blanket. But then the girls voted and decided that wasn't very nice, so Cynthia took it back.

But I gotta tell you, Stanley Washington has

been getting on my nerves lately. Maybe it's the way he's always mooching around Jared, acting like the two of them are so much tougher than Corey and Kevin and me. *And* he's sarcastic.

"Who says you're in charge?" my friend Kevin asks, challenging Stanley as the rest of the kids churn around them, pushing to get their snacks and escape outside. "You're not the boss of the kickballs, Stanley."

"He is if I say he is," Jared says, standing in the middle of the cubicle room like a rock sticking out of the ocean waves. "Anyway, what do you guys care?" he adds, including me in his glare, even though I haven't said a word. "You're gonna be too busy talking about how great *little sisters* are to play anything."

"Ooh," Stanley says, laughing. "Cute little Waffle."

"Her name's Alfie," I say, clenching my fists.

Waffle! That's it for me and sarcastic Stanley.

"Whatever," Jared says, shrugging as we make our way down the hall. "Sorry, but you guys are just too wimped-out to play with the kickballs today. Especially when we're playing Extreme Dodgeball, dudes."

Okay. Plain dodgeball is a real game. Everyone knows that. It has rules and everything, even though the rules can change from place to place. I happen to know this, because the official way we play it at Oak Glen, when we're being supervised by a playground monitor—and there's only one now—is not the same way they play it in high school, or even in middle school, for that matter. At Oak Glen, we use soft, bouncy kickballs, not real dodgeballs, and we follow the simplest rules. If you're hit full-on, without the ball bouncing first, and nobody on your team catches the ball before it hits the ground, you're o-u-t, out. For good.

But in the past couple of weeks, when no one is supervising us, **WATCH OUT!** Because if no grown-ups are around, the game has become what we now call Extreme Dodgeball. And it's very *unofficial.*

It's like dodgeball in a mirror, in fact. Everything is the opposite.

In plain, supervised dodgeball at my school, for instance, you can't kick the ball, or come back into the game once you're out—or be a bad sport, cheat, or hit the ball at someone's head. And the teams always start out even. But in Extreme

Dodgeball, you can do whatever you want.

So far, we haven't been caught, which is cool and scary at the same time.

"Grab a ball and start playing!" Kevin yells as all us boys erupt onto the rain-shiny playground, nutritious snacks forgotten. The playground monitor is way across the playground, helping some girl with a bloody nose, it looks like.

"EllRay, think fast!" Corey shouts, and he hurls a dark red ball in my direction.

I catch it like I have superpowered magnet hands, then I toss it into the air and spike it into Stanley's big plaid back as he hunches over the stretchy net filled with balls. **BOINK!** "You're out," I yell at Stanley, like we're playing plain dodgeball and following the rules.

Stanley just keeps playing, of course.

"*You're* out, loser," Jared yells, slamming a ball into my shoulder from just two feet away—which hurts enough to make me want to hurt someone back.

Kids aren't allowed to say "loser" at Oak Glen, by the way, but this is Extreme Dodgeball, so that's the least of anyone's worries. And anyway, I've already picked up a ball and bopped it back at Jared. "Take that!" I shout, like we're in a boxing ring and I just punched him one in the nose.

I pretend I can hear an invisible crowd cheer me on. "*Go, EllRay, go!*"

By now, the kickballs are flying all over the place, but we are just scooping them up and slamming them into some other kid, anyone who's playing. Even our own team members, and they're just laughing! And though Jared did get me that once, I'm pretty much escaping being hit. Just a couple of grazes is all.

See, there are some good things about being a small guy. I'm bouncing around the playground like I'm a kickball myself!

This is *so much fun*. When I'm racing around, dodging kickballs and looking for the next guy to bash, there's no Ms. Sanchez, no third grade, no playground rules. There's no Alfie or Suzette Monahan or hidden pink jacket or hurt feelings, either, much less Mom and Dad telling me to make good choices. I grab a bouncing ball and spike it at my target like a pro beach volleyball player.

KA-BLAM!

"Ow!" someone yells.

"Baby! " Jared shouts to the yeller, but then he shuts up fast, because it's his friend Stanley. And Stanley is holding his eye like there's something wrong.

His twisted glasses are lying at his feet.

"Time out," Kevin calls like it's just an ordinary game, and it's no one's fault that Stanley maybe got hurt.

But unfortunately, I know better.

10

A GOOD DEAL?

"Dude. You are so lucky," Kevin says to me after school for the third time since nutrition break.

"You don't have to keep telling me that," I say.

After they checked out Stanley Washington's eye in the office this morning, he ended up going home before lunch. But not because his eye was messed up. It wasn't. His glasses were. I mean the metal part that holds the glasses together.

The actual glasses were plastic, so they didn't break.

His mom could have brought his old pair of glasses to school, Ms. Sanchez told us, her voice icy because of what happened during nutrition break, but Stanley had a dentist appointment this afternoon, so his mother just picked him up late in the morning and they took off.

"But dude. Nobody saw you hit him except me," Kevin marvels. "It's like you were invisible!"

Invisible! Like Alfie. Maybe it runs in the family.

Stanley shouldn't have called Alfie "Waffle," that's what he shouldn't have done, I think, trying to come up with a good reason why it was Stanley's own fault he got hit.

Not that anyone except Kevin saw me spike the ball at Stanley's floppy-haired, glasses-wearing head.

"It's because I'm so short and fast," I say, shrugging. "It has its good points, I guess."

"Yeah," Kevin agrees, grinning. "Like sneaking around places, and creeping through fences, and getting away with stuff. Major stuff, like this."

I don't really like the way this is making me sound. "I'm not some *weasel*," I object.

"No," Kevin agrees hastily. "But you're a real good shot, EllRay. And that counts for a lot. Especially when no one sees you."

★ ★ ★

I'm not such a good shot as all that, I admit to myself half an hour later as I walk down our driveway. I mean, we were just playing a game, and it happened to be Extreme Dodgeball. And all us guys—including Stanley!—know Extreme Dodgeball doesn't have any rules, except to not get caught playing it, because it's too rough for school.

It's not my fault there's just one playground monitor now, is it?

But part of me remembers snagging that ball on purpose, eyeing Stanley's sarcastic, floppy-haired head, then tossing the ball into the air for a championship spike at just the right angle, glasses or no glasses.

Kickballs are soft rubber balls!

They're not supposed to be hard enough to hurt someone!

And they didn't. They hurt someone's *glasses*.

Anyway, Stanley should have been watching out.

"EllWay," a familiar voice calls from the kitchen door. "Why are you just standing there, looking at a twee?"

That's "tree" in Alfie-speak. You have probably cracked the code by now.

"I was thinking," I tell her. "We do that a lot in the third grade."

"And you can't think and walk at the same time," she says like she's just answered her own question. "Will you make me some toast?" she asks as she follows me into the kitchen.

Alfie's not allowed to use the toaster—not since that time she decided to heat up a slice of cheese in our old one. "Where's Mom?" I ask her, tossing my backpack onto a kitchen stool.

"She's working," Alfie reports. "She barely even heard me when I was talking to her."

Mom has been really busy with the latest fantasy book she's writing, and she gets so fuzzy, thinking about the people in the book, that she sometimes forgets about Alfie and me. Just a little. And that's weird, isn't it? For a kid's mom to wander around the house thinking about pretend people's problems when her own two kids have plenty of problems of their own?

Not that I mind taking charge. Which reminds me. "How did it go today?" I ask my little sister, popping two pieces of bread into the toaster. "Telling Suzette that you don't care what she does, but she should leave you alone, I mean?"

"It went perfect," Alfie says, smiling as she gets

a jar of peanut butter out of the fridge for her peanut butter and honey sandwich.

I'm in charge of the honey, because of that other time.

"So, you're not invisible anymore?" I ask, thinking suddenly of me and Stanley, and how no one but Kevin saw it when I stealth-spiked that ball at his head.

"No, I still am," Alfie says with a sigh, staring at the toaster as if that might hurry things up. "But she told me how I could break her magic spell."

Her magic spell. Great. "And how are you gonna do that?" I ask, waiting for it.

"By giving her something," Alfie tells me, matter-of-fact. "One of my dolls. And she gets to choose which one."

Okay. Alfie has a super-huge doll collection, it's true, but she loves every single one of them, *and* all their clothes and stuff. She makes up stories about them and everything. One of Alfie's dolls even has its own pink plastic pony.

"You're solving your problem by *giving* her something?" I repeat, trying not to yell at her. "But—but that's like Suzette's a robber, Alfie! She *is* a dragon, and she has you in her power. You cannot let her steal from you. Not one of your dolls. I—I *forbid* it."

"You're not the boss of me, EllWay Jakes," Alfie says, her brown eyes flashing. "And Suzette's not a dwagon," she adds. "And it's not stealing if I give her the doll my own self," she adds, like she's repeating an explanation someone else gave her.

Suzette Monahan, that's who. **GREEN** and ***SCALY*** Suzette, with her pinchy dragon face, her sharp, scratching claws, and her spiky, lashing tail.

"It's a good deal, EllWay," Alfie says, trying to convince me as the toast pops up.

"A good deal?" I say. I get the hot pieces of toast out of the toaster and start tossing them in my hands as I look for a plate. Alfie just stands there, holding her precious jar of peanut butter like it's filled with pirate jewels.

I have to do *everything* around here?

"It is *not* a good deal, it's a terrible deal," I tell Alfie. "What Suzette is doing is probably against the law, even! Or it should be. And you can eat your toast cold, if you're gonna let yourself get rooked by some goofy four-year-old robber. What do I care?" I say, flipping her toast onto the counter. "And you're not getting any honey for that sandwich, either."

Because—I give up. If Alfie doesn't have that getting-mad ingredient I've been trying to pass down to her after this latest stunt of Suzette's, she's a lost cause. Where's that famous Jakes pride Dad is always talking about?

Alfie can just go through her whole entire life being bullied, that's all.

She does not deserve a big brother like me.

"But we worked it all out like you told me to," Alfie wails, her peanut butter and honey sandwich forgotten for the moment. "And I won't be invisible *next week*. See, it's perfect now!"

"So," I say, arms folded across my chest like Dad does when one of us has done something really bad. "When is this great doll-choosing event gonna happen, Alfie? Because I want to see it with my very own eyes. I want to watch you get cheated by a bully."

"Well, you're not invited, and it's happening tomorrow," Alfie says, sniffling. "And you can't stop it, EllWay Jakes. Because—I don't want to be invisible no more!"

"*Any* more," I correct her.

"Oh, *s-word*," Alfie shouts at me, clear as can be.

She can go from sad to mad in one second flat. A world record, probably.

"*What* did you say?" I ask. I cannot believe my ears. If Mom or Dad heard her say the s-word, the world would probably explode. Our world would, anyway.

"That means *shut up*, in case you didn't know," Alfie informs me, grabbing her cold toast off the counter and clutching the two pieces to her chest, along with the jar of peanut butter.

This looks like "an accident about to happen," as my dad would say.

And now, Alfie's T-shirt with the frilly sleeves has crumbs all over it, which is not gonna fly once she sees them. Major clothes change coming up. "And I don't even care about the honey, *EllWay*," she tells me, still furious. "Because I like plain peanut butter, all by itself!"

Which is not true, by the way.

But we're way past telling the truth around here.

Alfie's pretending she's not about to be robbed by that slimy little dragon, Suzette Monahan, and I'm pretending I don't care.

"So, what if *I* start saying you're invisible, Alfie?" I ask, trying one last time. "Did you ever think of that? And what'll you give me to stop? See, it never ends!"

"It *will* end," Alfie says, stomping her foot hard on the kitchen floor. "It will end tomorrow afternoon, when Suzette comes over to play."

"To rob you, you mean," I say, turning away. "I can't *see* you!" I sing out, facing the empty corner of the room. "Who's that talking behind me? Someone invisible? Why, it's no one at all," I say, turning around.

"Liar, liar, liar!" Alfie yells, tears spurting from her eyes as she flees the kitchen.

Let her cry!

To *think* I spiked that extreme dodgeball at Stanley Washington's head because I was mad at him for calling Alfie a waffle! Well, I was mad at Stanley for a bunch of other reasons, too, but I forget what they are right now.

Us boys don't really know or care why we get mad at each other, in my opinion. We just do, and fast. Then we either get over it or fight, and that's that.

But girls save up every little detail when *they* get mad. Then the girls sit on their hurts like chickens guarding a bunch of golden eggs, and then they cluck about each egg for *weeks*. I've seen this happen in my class.

I don't remember exactly what it was that made me blow up at Stanley. Being mad at him seemed important at the time, though.

And it's all I had to work with back then.

11

BEING PROUD

Dad and I drive around doing chores on Saturday mornings. It's "our chance to catch up," he always says. But it's more him catching up with me than me catching up with him. The thing is, his geology work is about something called "isotope ratios," not just which rock is prettiest. So you can see why our catching up is so one-sided. Not even most grown-ups know what he's talking about.

I want my dad to be proud of me more than anything, but it's hard. He's a professor, which is like an extra-fancy teacher, and I'm just a shrimpy kid who is only medium-good at everything. When I'm even paying attention, that is.

I have trouble with that, too. There's a lot going on inside my head.

But I know this much. I do *not* want to do anything boring like a geology professor when I grow up! If I don't get to be a Laker, I want to be a stuntman, or else just a plain old millionaire, so nobody can tell me what to do. I think if you're rich enough, no one cares how short you are.

I will have a giant gumball machine—and the gum will be totally free!—in my fancy front hall that will be so big, you can skateboard in it. Also, I will have every video game known to mankind in my all-glass house. And I'll be able to eat popcorn whenever I want, even in the middle of the night. Maybe I'll hire a TV cooking star whose only job is to make really cool snacks for me and my—

"EllRay?" my dad says, sounding like he's just asked me something.

"Sorry," I reply. "What were you saying?"

"That we're almost at the nursery," he says, sounding happy to share this news with me.

On our Saturday mornings, we are usually on our way either to the plant nursery—for rose stuff—or to the hardware store. The plant nursery is a zero, in my opinion, except for all the cool poisons in the **STINKY** aisle. But the hardware store is an excellent place to plan your next Halloween costume. They have all sizes of chains on big spools, though I can't figure out yet how to use them in a costume. And they also have space invader–type masks, and stretchy vent tubes you could use for robot arms, especially if you spray-painted them silver.

True, it is only April, but you cannot start planning too soon for Halloween.

At our hardware store, there is also a big gray cat with a chewed-up ear living there who likes to sleep on top of a big stack of doormats. It's fun seeing him, because we don't have any pets at home. Alfie's allergic. "And then we'll go to the hardware store?" I ask, trying not to jinx it by sounding too hopeful.

"Sure," Dad says. "There's always *something* we need there. And then. . . ."

He draws out these last two words in a tempting way, a smiles big at me, because me and my dad share one small secret.

Our Saturday morning doughnut!

I smile back at him. "Chocolate sprinkles," I tell him. "I have a question," I add, surprising even myself. "It's about being proud. You're always saying Alfie and I should be proud of ourselves.

So that means pride's a good thing, right?"

"It *can* be a good thing, even though pride—vanity, that is—is considered to be one of the seven big vices," Dad says, after thinking about it for a couple of seconds. "And not a 'vise' like in the hardware store, son. This 'vice' is spelled with a C in the middle, and it's something bad."

My dad explains everything way too much. That can be frustrating, especially if you're in a hurry. But it also means that you always know he has listened to your question and taken it seriously.

"Wait. What?" I ask, now totally confused in the back seat. "So is pride a good thing or a bad thing?"

"Well," Dad says, stopping at a red light, which is always a good idea, "if you're so proud that you think you're a better, smarter, or nicer-looking kid than anyone else you know, that's a bad thing. But if you're proud enough to know you're as *good* as everyone else, that you try to be the best you can be, that's a good thing."

"Corey Robinson's a lot better swimmer than I'll ever be," I tell my dad.

"Do you feel proud of him?" Dad asks.

"Yeah," I say. "I mean, I wish I was better at

swimming than I am, but I'm proud Corey's a champion. I like to brag about him."

"See, *that's* a good kind of pride, too," my dad tells me as we pull into the crowded plant nursery parking lot. "And if your swimming improved even a little bit, it would be a good thing to be proud of that. We can work on it next summer, if you want."

"Maybe," I say with some caution, because my dad can go overboard when he helps me work on stuff. Last year, when I said I *might* like to be a Cub Scout, mostly because Kevin was talking about joining, the next thing I knew I was wearing a uniform with too-big blue shorts sagging down below my knees, and I was reciting some pledge. When the whole thing was just an idea that had floated across my brain.

And Kevin never even joined!

Nothing against the Cub Scouts.

"But can you *teach* someone to be proud? Someone little?" I ask my dad as if it's just an ordinary question. Like I'm not talking about Alfie.

"To have pride in himself, you mean? I hope your mother and I did that with you," Dad says as he wrestles a giant shopping cart loose from a big tangle of them. You should see these carts. They're double-deckers. You could ride in the bottom of one, if your dad let you. I could, anyway.

"Or pride in *her*self," I say, not looking at him.

"Well, sure," Dad says, sounding a little lost in this conversation. And being lost anytime, anywhere, is unusual for him.

"But you can't just keep telling them and telling them to 'show a little pride,' because that doesn't work," I say, just barely keeping it from coming out like a question.

"I suppose not," Dad says, distracted now by a display of rose bushes in dark plastic pots.

Right after Christmas, these same plants were what Dad called "bare root roses," and they looked like a bunch of thorny sticks poking out of dirt-filled burlap bags. They hadn't started growing any leaves or flowers then. But the nursery still charged money for them.

With bare root roses, Dad told me, you just have to assume something good is gonna happen.

But he decided to wait until now before he bought any. That's how careful he is.

Dad picks up one of the rose bushes and examines its metal tag. "Telling someone to 'show some pride' would have been like commanding a bare root rose to 'show some flowers, and make it snappy' last Christmas, I suppose," he adds, sliding me a look. "When it was just too soon in the year for that to happen."

"I didn't say I'd *command* them," I object, looking away.

"The roses you see now existed somewhere deep inside those roots, the way pride exists somewhere in Alfie," Dad says, placing a rose bush on our cart

with so much care that it makes me feel jealous for a second. "And if we had planted one of those bare root roses correctly last January, say, and taken good care of it, the flowers would have emerged in their own good time. We wouldn't have had to teach that bare root rose a thing, just the way we won't need to tell this rose bush what to do. Or tell your little sister how to be her bravest and truest self."

"Huh," I say, not really convinced—because he doesn't know Alfie.

Well, he *does* know Alfie. Obviously. She's his kid.

And maybe Alfie *is* a little like a bare root rose. And maybe the right kind of pride will burst out of her some day—probably along with a lot more thorns.

But Dad does not know that she's about to make a fool of herself—or that now, she has no pride at all, even though he and Mom are taking very good care of her.

So I'm gonna have to step in—step up, *man up*—and defend my little sister.

Suzette Monahan, here comes **ELLRAY JAKES THE DRAGON SLAYER!**

12

UPROAR

"Eat a little more of your sandwich, sweetheart," Mom tells Alfie at lunch, after Dad and I have gotten back from doing our Saturday morning chores.

"Or eat *some*, at least," my dad chimes in, looking at Alfie's tuna sandwich, which has been trimmed down to four triangles with the crusts cut off. It's barely there. "Your friend Suzanne will be here in less than an hour."

"It's *Suzette*, Warren," my mom whispers, sounding shocked, as if maybe the dreaded Suzette can hear this terrible mistake from wherever it is she lives in Oak Glen.

On Green and Scaly Lane, maybe.

"Oh. Excuse *me*," my dad says, trying to be funny. But really, all of us—except for Dad, who I don't think remembers the story of Suzette's one other visit to our house—are feeling weird about

Suzette coming over again, but each for our own reasons.

Alfie probably feels weird because she wants everything to go perfectly, so she can spend the rest of her life as a visible human being.

I think Mom feels weird because she loves Alfie, and she knows this playdate is important to her. But Mom also doesn't want to have a bossy four-year-old like Suzette giving her any grief about snacks, or wrecking everything by demanding to be taken home early if she doesn't get her way.

And I feel weird because I know what's really up, that Suzette is basically planning to steal one of Alfie's best dolls. *And* because I have a secret two-part plan to keep Alfie from giving in to Suzette, only I'm not sure if I can pull it off. See, I've already had some experience with her.

"Alfie, eat something," Mom is saying again.

Alfie is still drooped over her sandwich. In an instant, I realize what the problem is. Alfie told me once that after she'd brought a tuna sandwich to the "Welcome, Kreative Learners!" picnic, Suzette told kids that she smelled like cat food. Alfie must be worried about smelling like a cat again.

"Can I eat Alfie's tuna sandwich—because I'm so hungry?" I ask, reaching for my little sister's plate. "I'll make Alfie a peanut butter and honey sandwich. She's way too excited for tuna."

This makes no sense at all, but no one calls me on it, even though the whole making-whatever-you-want-for-lunch thing goes against family rules.

But this is a special occasion, I guess. Mom seems to think so, anyway. "I suppose you can," she says, her forehead wrinkling as she looks at my dad, who just shrugs his agreed permission.

Alfie gives me a look so full of thanks—as I cram one of her sandwich triangles into my mouth and get to work—that I feel even madder at Suzette Monahan than I did before, if that's possible.

And that stinky little dragon hasn't even gotten here yet!

★ ★ ★

"Go away. You're a boy," Suzette Monahan tells me from Alfie's shaggy rug, where she and Alfie are lining up Alfie's dolls like the dolls are in a contest.

I guess they are. Which unlucky doll will Suzette take home?

"Big duh, I'm a boy," I say. "Do you think I don't know that already?"

"That's my brother EllWay," Alfie tells Suzette, as if she hopes things will calm down after this introduction. "He's eight," she adds, trying to make me sound important.

Alfie's voice sounds different when she is talking to Suzette, I notice at once. Softer, worried, and like what she's saying is about to turn into a question.

"I don't care. Make him go away, or I'm leaving," Suzette says, narrowing her green eyes as she glares at me.

Amazingly enough, Suzette Monahan looks like a regular four-year-old, I think, standing in the doorway and staring at her. She has curly brown hair that is smoother in front than it is on top, as if she only brushes the parts she can see. She is taller than Alfie, and very thin. She reminds me of a grasshopper, crouched on Alfie's rug that way. She flexes her hands as if she's about to spring at me and start scratching.

"EllWay?" Alfie asks, giving me the please-please-please look that usually works.

Sorry, Alfie. Not this time.

"Mom wants you in the kitchen," I tell my little sister. "To help her make a special snack."

Alfie turns to Suzette. "You come too," she says, almost begging. "Maybe we'll get to fwost something."

Like there's going to be frosting. No, Mom is making chocolate chip cookies. And Suzette is either going to like them, or she'll go home hungry. I don't care.

"I'm busy," Suzette says, not even looking at Alfie. She picks up two dolls, one in each claw, I mean *hand*, and jiggles them a little, like she's weighing them or something. "Hmm," she says, tilting her head.

She's choosing which doll to steal from Alfie right in front of me!

"Go on. Mom's waiting," I tell Alfie, not taking my eyes off Suzette.

And so Alfie hurries down the hall.

It is time for me to begin my two-part plan.

Part one involves talking to Suzette like she's a normal person.

HA HA HA HA HA!

That's funny because—would a normal person mess up another person's bookcase, and then put a tutu on his soldier action figure? That's not just rude, it's unpatriotic! And would a normal person talk back to another person's mom the way Suzette did that time? Not to mention what she's doing to Alfie at Kreative Learning? And doing here, now, in our very own house? But I should at least try.

"Look, Suzette," I say. "You have to stop bullying my little sister. Period."

"No, I don't," she says, sounding calm as she examines two other dolls. "Besides, bullying's against the law."

"You're doing it anyway," I inform her. As if she didn't know.

"You're not the boss of me," she says.

I think that must be four-year-olds' favorite thing to say, and it's *so* not true. Nearly everyone is the boss of them. Or they should be.

"You're a bully if you hurt other kids' feelings for no reason," I tell Suzette. "And also if you make other girls go along with you. Girls like—like Moany and Gnarly," I say, wishing for the first time in my life that I'd paid attention to Alfie's babbling so I could remember her other friends' real names.

But Suzette must get the idea.

"*Mona and Arletty*," Suzette corrects me, a tiny smile turning up at the corners of her skinny dragon mouth for the first time. "You just made fun of them! They'll be real mad, Alfie's Brother. Even at *Alfie*, maybe."

And—she reaches for another doll. The doll who has the pink plastic pony.

"This is your last chance to stop bullying Alfie, Suzette Monahan," I say, lowering my voice the way Dad does when he means business.

"Go away, Alfie's Brother, or I'm gonna take *two* dolls," Suzette says, not even looking up. "Or Alfie's new pink jacket."

The pink jacket Alfie won't even wear anymore.

Suzette *is* terrible! See?

It is time for part two of my plan to protect my little sister.

13

BABYISH

"Too bad about that bed-wetting thing you do," I say, trying to sound as bored as she does. "That's so babyish for a four-year-old. Ooh, smelly little baby."

I have totally made this up.

Suzette finally looks at me, her hands still. "What?" she asks, frowning.

"I've heard all about it," I say. "Not from Alfie," I add quickly. "She's too nice to say something that personal about a friend. But other kids might find out," I tell her, shrugging.

"I do *not* wet my bed," Suzette says, her cheeks turning just pink enough with anger to tell me that she might. Every so often, at least.

"Sure, you do," I say.

"Don't say that," Suzette says, throwing down Alfie's doll and covering her ears.

"Okay," I tell her real loud, shrugging again. "But that just proves it's true. So *babyish*," I say again.

Suzette's mouth is just a straight pink line. "**LIAR-LIAR-PANTS-ON-FIRE**," she finally tells me, but her voice wobbles. "Who cares what you say?"

"Lots of people," I say, lowering my voice. "Starting with my friend Corey's little sister, and Jared's little brother, just to name two. They both go to Kreative Learning, and I'm sure they'll spread the news all around."

"They're just babies," Suzette says, her green eyes flashing with anger. But she's relaxing a little, probably thinking my threat is pretty weak. "They can barely talk."

"Ah. But you'll be going to Oak Glen Primary School pretty soon," I remind her. "Next year, right? For kindergarten? And that news will be waiting for you, because I'm gonna tell *everyone*. Unless you stop bullying Alfie, that is. 'Here comes Suzette-Monahan-the-bed-wetter!' they'll all say," I tell her, as if making an announcement.

Now, I have her complete attention.

Do I feel mean? Yeah, a little. Maybe a lot. But I have to defend my sister.

"It's a big fat lie," Suzette says, the words almost exploding out of her mouth.

I shrug again. "So is telling other kids that Alfie's invisible," I point out. "That's a lie too, isn't it?"

"Huh," she says, almost snorting out the word like a stinky puff of dragon smoke.

"I guess some people tell lies," I say, shrugging for the third time. "But at least I have a reason for lying, Suzette. Unlike you."

"It's still not right," she mutters, and I guess she's correct about that.

But I can live with being a little wrong. It's for a good cause.

The sweet smell of baking cookies floats down the hall, which seems weird, given the sour things going on in Alfie's pink and purple room.

"Lying is *wrong*," Suzette says, trying to sound like the queen of good behavior. But her pointy chin is wobbling just enough to remind me that she is only four years old, and I feel kinda bad again for a second.

She's been picking on Alfie since forever, though, hasn't she?

"I know it's wrong," I say quietly. "So I'll quit lying if you will."

"You're still gonna tell," Suzette says, narrowing her dragon eyes once more. "Just for the fun of it. Mean *boy.*"

"Is that why you lied about Alfie being invisible?" I ask. "For the fun of it?"

Now, Suzette is the one to shrug. "I don't know," she mumbles.

I think she's actually telling the truth, for once.

"But you're going to quit it?" I ask again.

Suzette doesn't say anything right away, but she gives one of Alfie's newest dolls a reluctant pat, as if telling it good-bye. "You can't make me *like* Alfie," she finally says. "You're still not the boss of me."

"I don't want to be the boss of you," I say, meaning it, except for where Alfie is concerned. "And I don't care if you like her or not," I add. "Just treat her fair, that's all. Like any other kid. And leave the other girls alone if they want to play with her. I'll hear about it if you don't."

"Go away, Alfie's Brother," Suzette says, sounding more tired than angry now. "I wanna go home."

"You can go home when my mom says you can," I inform her. "And no stealing any of Alfie's dolls at the last minute, either, not to mention her jacket, or the deal is off. Tell Alfie you changed your mind about wanting anything."

I can hear pink-sneakered footsteps **THUDDING** down the hall. "The cookies are ready," Alfie tells us, screeching to a halt just outside her bedroom door. "Come and eat 'em while they're still all warm and melty! With icy-cold milk!"

"You guys go ahead," I tell Alfie and Suzette. "Mom will save me a few."

"Suzette?" Alfie says, her voice turning soft with worry once more.

"Sure. I guess," Suzette says, getting to her feet. "But they better be good."

She sneaks me a questioning look when she says this last mean thing, but I just ignore her, turning away.

With some kids, I think mean is kind of a habit. Maybe they can't stop it that fast.

"EllWay?" Alfie says, putting her little golden hand on my arm. "Are you all wight? Because—*chocolate chips.*"

Chocolate is Alfie's favorite food group.

"I'm fine, Alfie," I say. "I've just got some stuff I have to do. *Boy* stuff," I add.

Like lying down flat on my bedroom floor while I try to recover from my dragon-slaying ordeal.

Man, that was *hard.* Every single bone in my body is aching, and I actually have a headache from threatening Suzette Monahan with a really mean lie.

But it was *so-o-o* worth it.

14

AN UNUSUALLY QUIET DINNER

"This smells funny," Alfie says, poking at her grilled cheese sandwich.

"No, it doesn't," Mom informs her, sounding tired.

It is an unusually quiet dinner tonight. It's the kind of dinner a family has after driving two hours to have lunch with relatives they barely know, because "family is important." Or it's what dinner would be like after taking your little sister to the emergency room after she fell off the slide at the park one afternoon, and then you had to sit in the waiting room for more than two hours with a bunch of scary-looking people, some of them bleeding, even. But your sister was fine.

Mom heated up a can of soup tonight and made grilled cheese sandwiches, that's how worn out she is. Usually, Saturday dinners are a big deal around here.

Chicken with mashed potatoes. Spaghetti and meatballs. That kind of thing.

But we have all had too much Suzette Monahan for this to be a regular night.

Some people are energy vampires, that's what I think.

Alfie usually loves grilled cheese, but tonight she is eyeballing her sandwich like she suspects there's something weird inside. Eggplant, maybe.

Dad is pretty quiet at dinner most of the time, apart from asking us about our best things and worst things of the day, one of our family customs. I guess he has a lot to think about, with all the rocks there are in this world.

But tonight, he left the dining room to take a phone call, even though usually, the rule is no phone calls during dinner.

As for me, I still have a headache from telling that lie. And what was the lie? It was *threatening* Suzette Monahan about the bed-wetting thing, because I wouldn't really have told anyone. Who would be interested?

"It *does* smell funny," Alfie insists, giving her sandwich another angry jab.

"Don't eat it, then," Mom says, shrugging.

Alfie looks up, shocked. "But I'll starve," she says, and my mom actually starts to laugh. I do too, because while Alfie isn't fat, she's not skinny, either. She is in-between, with a button popping off every so often. "It's not funny," Alfie says, heating up. "Stop laughing!"

"We're laughing *with* you, not *at* you," Mom assures her, even though Alfie isn't laughing.

I don't really see the difference between these two things when Mom says that to me, but Alfie buys it. "Well, *okay*," she says with a sniff.

"I thought you'd be happy tonight, Alfie," I say, stirring my soup in slow circles with a spoon. "You got everything you wanted. Your friend Suzette came over. And you guys had a yummy snack," I continue, "and Suzette left here *empty-handed*," I add, trying to give Alfie a meaningful look. But Alfie is still glaring down at her grilled cheese sandwich, which is now probably more of an orange glue sandwich, it's so cold.

"Oh, EllRay, no guest leaves this house empty-

handed," Mom objects, trying to work up some of her usual pep. "I gave Suzette a nice big bag of chocolate chips cookies to share with her family."

I try to imagine a family of pinchy-faced brunette dragons fighting over those chocolate chip cookies, claws scratching, crumbs and green scales flying, but my little sister's sad face gets in the way. "So what's the matter?" I ask.

Alfie shrugs. "I dunno," she says softly as Mom

goes into the kitchen to refill the water pitcher.

Alfie and I are alone in the dining room. "Didn't you have fun today?" I ask.

"Kind of," she tells me. "Suzette even let me keep all my dolls."

"Amazing," I say.

"See, that's how nice she is," Alfie tries to explain.

"Suzette's not *nice*, Alfie," I say, shaking my head. "Just because she didn't rob you, that doesn't mean she's—"

"And she'll let me be visible again next week," Alfie continues, looking relieved.

"Big whoop. You always *were* visible," I say. "If you can't see that yourself, I don't know how you expect me help you."

"But I never asked you to help me," Alfie says, scowling. "And I didn't ask you to wreck my play date, either, EllWay. No wonder Suzette doesn't like me," she adds, loud enough for only me to hear.

"She said that?" I ask.

"Kinda," Alfie says. "Not in words, but I could tell. She thought I was a baby, with my big brother busting in and ruining things."

I can tell that the more she repeats this, the truer it will sound to her.

Alfie may really be a beautiful-rose-about-to-happen, but she has a ways to go. So far, she's still mostly bare roots and a few thorns.

Well, let her think what she wants. Maybe she needs to have an excuse why Suzette Monahan doesn't like her!

"It's your fault," Alfie says.

"Ooh, somebody's tired," Mom says, coming back into the dining room and sitting down again.

"Somebody is *not* tired," Alfie says, pouting. "Somebody is starving, that's all. I want a hot dog for dinner. Or a cheese pizza just for me."

"This isn't a restaurant," Mom says. "You'll eat what's in front of you or hope for better luck next time."

Alfie and I just sit there like two frozen kid-sicles, because—that's what Mom's grandma used to say to *her*, when she was little. My mom's *grouchy* grandma. The stories about her always scare me a little.

And now Mom's saying the same thing to us!

"And speaking of 'better luck next time,'" my dad says, entering the dining room with his empty sandwich plate, "I need to speak to you, EllRay Jakes. Now. In my office."

"Oh, Warren, can't it wait?" Mom says, tossing her napkin onto the table in defeat, as if now, even this skimpy, interrupted Saturday night dinner has been wrecked.

"I'm afraid not, Louise," Dad says, still standing in the doorway. "It's a very serious matter."

"Oh, no," Alfie whispers. "Poor *EllWay*."

"It's okay," I whisper back, touching my little sister's shoulder as I pass her chair.

Suzette must have **BLABBED**. Like I said before, though, it was worth it, standing up for my little sister.

"But it's a very serious matter!" Alfie says, as if I needed reminding.

"EllRay?" my dad says, still waiting by the door.

"Coming," I say.

☼ 15 ☼

MIRROR LAND

"Sit down, son," Dad tells me when we're inside his office, and he has closed the door.

It's strange, but my dad calls me "son" most often when I'm in trouble. So as I perch on the edge of the chair near his desk, I try to figure out how to explain the whole Suzette Monahan thing to him in just the right way. Not like I'm making excuses, or trying to get credit for something or, worse, lying, because my father is like a living, breathing lie detector.

I just want to tell the story in a way that makes me look good.

Also, I don't want him to go nuts and start forming committees about Alfie being bullied at Kreative Learning. I think that problem, at least, has been solved.

Suzette! *That little green tattletale.*

"So. I just got off the phone with Mr. Washington," Dad tells me.

"*George* Washington?" I ask, really amazed for part of one second.

I don't know what makes me say "George Washington." It's probably because we have been learning the presidents. Also, Dad surprised me with his announcement. I thought we were going to be talking about Suzette Monahan!

"Don't try to be funny with me, Lancelot Raymond Jakes," my father says, his eyebrows lowering. Never a good sign.

Okay. Lancelot Raymond is my real name, which is obviously why I changed it to EllRay as soon as I could talk.

First, it was L-period-Ray for short, but now, it's just plain EllRay.

"I'm not trying to be funny," I tell Dad, my voice shaking. "That just kind of popped out. But—who's Mr. Washington?"

"Stanley's father?" my dad says, making his answer a question. "Stanley Washington, from your third grade class at Oak Glen Primary School? *That* Mr. Washington? I was mortified."

"Mortified" means embarrassed plus ashamed, Dad explained to me once.

Ashamed. That's the *opposite* of proud, which is what I have been aiming for with my dad.

Good job, EllRay!

"But why would Mr. Washington call *you*?" I ask, still confused.

My dad looks at me in silence for a few seconds before he speaks. "How you can ask me that question after bullying his son Stanley is beyond me, EllRay. Why did you do it, son?"

Okay. My dad and I have now entered the mirror land of opposites. We are officially "over there," to use Alfie's term for being on the other side of the mirror.

Because—me, bully Stanley? It's more the other way around! Not that Stanley actually *bullies* me. Not like on TV specials or in the movies, and not even the way Suzette has been being mean to Alfie at Kreative Learning. Stanley and I don't like each other much lately, but that's about it.

My face is getting hot, I'm so angry.

Did Dad even ask me if I bullied Stanley? No. He asked *why* I did it.

"I never bullied anyone," I tell my father. "I *fight* bullies. I battle them. But you believe a stranger on the phone the minute he says something bad about me? Just because he's a *grown-up*?"

For the first time since I sat down, I see doubt in my father's eyes. "You're saying this didn't happen?" he asks. "That you didn't deliberately break Stanley's eyeglasses? And that you haven't been going after that poor kid for weeks, just for the heck of it? Because that's what Stanley told his father."

That poor kid? Poor, nearly-twice-as-big-as-me, name-calling, sarcastic Stanley?

DOINK! DOINK! DOINK! I can still hear Stanley saying that when Ms. Sanchez called on me in class that time when I wasn't paying attention.

He loves making me look bad in front of everyone!

And calling my little sister "Waffle?" *Hello?*

"No, I did not do any of those things!" I tell my dad, my heart thudding hard in my chicken-bone chest. "I don't know why, but he's lying. Well, except I did break his glasses," I admit, since someone must have seen me do it.

Someone besides Kevin, I mean. Because Kevin wouldn't tell on me.

But I wasn't *bullying* Stanley, I was getting even. There's a difference.

"So, you broke his eyeglasses," Dad says, latching onto that one bad thing.

"But it happened totally by accident," I say, stretching the truth a little. "*Almost* totally. We were playing dodgeball, see. We were all goofing around. Playing!" Yeah, okay. I aimed at Stanley. But like I already said, I'm not that good a shot.

"I'm sorry if I jumped to any conclusions, son," Dad says, staring at me with his dark brown eyes. "Maybe my surprise at receiving the call got the better of me. And my pride was hurt, hearing him say those things about you. You're my *son.* But eyeglasses don't grow on trees, you know. They can be very expensive."

"Stanley has another pair, Dad. Ms. Sanchez said so," I tell my father, knowing one second later that it was the wrong thing to say.

"That's beside the point," Dad says, shaking his

head. "The eyeglasses you broke were his newest prescription."

"Prescription?" I ask, confused. "Like for pills?"

"Like for pills," he says, nodding.

"But it was the *kickball* that broke Stanley's glasses, not me," I argue, again knowing at once that I've made another mistake.

Never try to argue with Dr. Warren Jakes. That's my advice to you.

"The big issue here is the alleged *bullying*, not the eyeglasses," Dad informs me, leaning back in his special desk chair and folding his arms across his chest. "Which is why Stanley Washington and his father are coming over to the house."

"When?" I ask, wondering how long it takes, and how much money it costs, for an eight-year-old kid to hire a lawyer.

Because *my own father* sure isn't sticking up for me.

"Tonight," Dad says. "In fact, they should be here any minute. Stanley's father very generously said he thought we should try to straighten this bullying thing out ourselves, before dragging the school into it. But if Stanley has been lying, we can get to the bottom of that, tonight, too."

Huh. Fat chance, I tell myself. Because if there's one thing Stanley Washington does not do, it is back down. I think Jared taught him that special skill. Stanley went four whole days once, saying that lima beans could grow in your stomach. And he still thinks hummingbirds die if they stop flying, even for a second. And I've *seen* them just sitting around.

"But what if Stanley keeps on lying?" I ask my dad, a hopeless feeling settling into my own lima bean–free stomach. "Are you gonna believe him, and not me? Just because he's a *stranger*?"

"Simmer down, son," Dad says. "We'll sort this out, I promise. But at the very least, you're going to have to pay for a new pair of eyeglasses for Stanley. Out of your allowance, EllRay—if it takes all year long."

"*Why?*" I ask.

"Because you're the one who broke them. You admitted it."

"It was an accident!" I say again. "At *recess*!"

There is a soft **KNOCK KNOCK** at Dad's office door. "Warren?" my mom says, peeking in. Her acorn-brown eyes are filled with concern, and I wish I could run to her for protection, or for a hug, at least. She believes in me no matter what. "Stanley Washington and his father are here to see you. Stanley's dad says you're expecting them?"

"We are," Dad says, including me in those two words. "I'll fill you in later, Louise," he adds, giving my mom a look that says, *Don't worry. It'll be all right.*

I wish he'd give *me* that look!

But oh, no. He's too busy believing a couple of strangers—and being *mortified* by me, his own son.

When all I ever wanted was to make him proud.

16

BULLY MATERIAL

"Please sit down. Make yourselves comfortable," Dad tells Mr. Washington and Stanley after a few silent moments. We have been standing in our living room like penguins, each of us rocking back and forth in his own spot.

It's like we're in a play, only nobody knows his lines.

I've never been in this much trouble before, that's the thing.

I guess Alfie has been hustled off to the family room. I can hear Itty Bitty Kitties singing their lame theme song.

Man, I wish I was in there with her.

Stanley won't look at me. He is squinting behind a pair of glasses that look too small for his big, floppy-haired head.

"Louise is making us some cocoa," Dad says,

pointing out chairs and sofas where Stanley and his dad can sit.

"Dude," Stanley whispers really fast, when his dad and my dad are finally next to each other on the sofa, busy making room on the low table in front of them for Mom's cocoa. "Sorry I lied about you breaking my glasses, but my dad blew up big-time when he heard I wrecked them again," he says. "And so I made up a bunch of stuff about how you've been going after me for a long time at school. You know, to get him off my back. So just go along with it, okay?"

"*What?*" I whisper back. "Go along with it? Are you kidding me?"

So, Stanley thinks he made the whole thing up! He doesn't know I really did it!

And I confessed to Dad about breaking Stanley's glasses when I didn't have to!

But I can kind of see why Stanley's afraid of his dad. Stanley's father is one of those big, smiley guys with not-smiling eyes who look like they're about to explode at any minute, still grinning away. I saw a bad guy like that once in a scary movie.

Mr. Washington is wearing a plaid shirt, too, like the kind Stanley always wears to school when it's cold out. I guess plaid runs in their family.

My dad doesn't look the slightest bit scared of Mr. Washington, I'm glad to say. Dad doesn't even look gloomy, like a guy who's about to be forced to apologize for something bad his doofus son did. Instead, he looks friendly and businesslike, like he called this meeting himself for some whole other reason.

"Let's wait for the cocoa to come before we begin," Dad says, being the boss. Stanley chooses a chair, then I take one as far away from him as possible.

While we're waiting, Dad looks from me to Stanley, then back at me again. Then, so does Mr. Washington, as if my dad's magnetic gaze has made him do the same thing.

There's me, with my skinny legs swinging because they don't reach the floor.

DOINK! DOINK! DOINK!

And there's big, hulking Stanley slumped in his chair like a boxer resting in his corner between rounds. Somehow he is managing to fidget at the same time that he's slumping, and one huge, sneakered foot is kicking at the chair leg.

And I feel embarrassed, because—maybe Dad didn't know I was such a pipsqueak until he saw me next to Stanley with his very own eyes!

My dad should see Jared, if he thinks *Stanley's* big.

It's not like I'm an elf and Stanley's a giant. It's not *that* huge a difference, but I think Mr. Washington is getting the silent point my dad is probably trying to make.

That is, I'm not exactly bully material.

Uh-oh. I hope Stanley's not gonna get it when they go home.

I'm glad Mom can't see him kicking her chair, though. It's one of her favorites.

Yes, ladies have favorite chairs.

My favorite chair is any place I can sit and eat a messy snack like nachos or pizza without getting yelled at.

"You okay over there, little guy?" Dad asks me, smiling.

"I'm fine," I peep, going along with it.

He has never called me "little guy" before, but he is obviously trying to strengthen his point.

Mom comes into the living room carrying a tray with four steaming cups of cocoa on it. And even though this is a terrible night, my mouth starts to water—because my mom makes really great cocoa. She doesn't use instant powder or anything, that's how good she is. She just *makes* it. I don't know how.

Dad jumps to his feet to help with the tray. "You'd like to join us, wouldn't you?" he asks my mom, in spite of the fact that there are only four cups of cocoa on the tray, not five.

"Oh, I think I'll just go keep Alfie company for a while," Mom says. "And then it'll be time for her bath."

And she hurries out of the room. Not that I blame her.

"Alfie is EllRay's little sister," Stanley informs his smiley-scary father. "She's only four years old. EllRay says that sometimes, it's *hard* being a big brother. He has to teach her stuff."

That's all from my personal narrative, of course, because I never told Stanley anything about my life. Why would I?

But—who knew he was paying that much attention?

Stanley's dad gives him a look. "Thanks for the info," he says, not sounding like he means it. "Now, come get your cocoa, Stanley—if you can manage not to spill it all over the place."

I think that Mr. Washington—"Plaid Dad," I've started calling him in my head—has already shifted over to our side, he seems so irked with Stanley. I guess he has figured out the truth, or at least some of it.

It's like Plaid Dad came into our house with an

invisible army behind him, he was so much in the right, but now the army is standing behind my dad.

And I think big liar Stanley really *is* about to splash cocoa all over the place, because his hands are shaking.

I actually feel sorry for him.

"I *did* break Stanley's glasses when we were playing," I announce in a too-loud voice that surprises even me, and probably my dad, too. "It was an accident," I say, "but I'm sorry anyway. And I'll pay him back for a brand-new pair of glasses—out of my own money," I add, those last words almost choking me.

Because it's not like I get some huge allowance or anything.

Stanley just gapes at me.

For all he knows, I confessed to this whole thing just to save his sorry bootie from the wrath of Plaid Dad.

Maybe I'll be Stanley's hero, now! That would be weird. Fun, but weird.

"Actually," my dad says to Plaid Dad, "I'll write you a check for the glasses when you know what the new pair will cost. And then EllRay will pay *me* back, bit by bit. And again, he's very sorry."

Stanley takes a noisy slurp of cocoa, then puts down his cup on a small table with a bang. He is staring at me with admiring eyes that are saying *thank-you-thank-you-thank-you*. "Dude," he says in a quiet, respectful voice.

He must think I'm handing over my allowance just to get him out of trouble!

"Well, thanks for that," Plaid Dad says, like he's sorry to have to surrender the words. "I'm guessing that Stanley may have exaggerated the rest of his story. You know, about being bullied for weeks by EllRay, over there," he adds probably hating to give up those words, too.

"I guess. Maybe," Stanley mumbles from across the room.

"It's easy to get carried away when you're trying to explain something," Dad says, trying to give Stanley a way out. "But my son is no bully."

"Obviously," Plaid Dad says with a chuckle, looking me up and down.

Wait. *Obviously?*

Dad clears his throat and sets his cup on the table in a careful way that tells me he's about to lose it. This is something that hardly ever happens.

He does not want anyone insulting me, or even my size.

He *is* proud of me, especially now that he knows the truth!

"I think we've just about covered everything," Dad says, standing up. Probably only I can hear how tight his voice has gotten, which is another bad sign with him.

And, as if my dad has made them do it, Stanley and his father stand up too, despite their almost-full cups of cocoa. "We'll be leaving, I guess," Plaid Dad says, looking around for his jacket.

"It's in the hall closet," Dad tells him, his voice extra-polite, but cool. "I'll tell Louise you said good-bye," he adds, sliding Mr. Washington's coat off its hanger.

"She's probably busy with Alfie," Stanley says, like he's the expert on our family.

But his eyes are still shining with relief as Dad opens our front door and the cold night air **WHOOSHES** in.

"Thanks," Stanley whispers as his dad is shaking my dad's hand, which I guess is something grown-ups do even when they don't like each other very much.

Or at all.

"It's okay," I tell Stanley.

"I'm sorry about your allowance," Stanley says, making a face.

"I'll live," I say, shrugging like it's no big deal.

It *is* a big deal, but I *will* live.

I'm just glad I'm not Stanley.

I mean, poor him!

17

AN APOLOGY

Alfie always goes to bed before I do, of course, since she's only four years old. It takes Mom a long time to settle her down. There are a lot of stories, cuddles, drinks of water, and trips to the bathroom involved. Sometimes Dad has to step in and say, "*Good night, Alfleta,*" in his deepest professor voice to put an end to it.

Bedtime is much easier with me. Mom usually reads a chapter or two from a book that's too hard for me to read alone, or she reads one that I want to hear again, but with my eyes closed. She doesn't cuddle me as much as she used to, though, because I'm eight. My call.

Boys grow out of that stuff faster than girls, I think. I don't know. It's not like I'm about to take a survey and ask the kids in my class, is it?

My dad usually pokes his head in my doorway

and booms out a "Night, EllRay! Don't let the bed-bugs bite." But we don't really have any bedbugs at our house. That's just an expression.

Tonight, though, I have gone to bed earlier than usual. I'm still worn out from Stanley's dad coming over to accuse me in person of being a bully, and from my dad's anger, and also from my secret battle with Suzette Monahan.

I just want today to be *over*. Sleep can do that for you, and it's free. Right now, Mom is still busy herding Alfie from her bedroom to the bathroom, then back again, with lots of chatter all along the way, so I guess there won't be any reading tonight. I'll probably be asleep before Alfie, which is just—**MORTIFYING**.

"EllRay?" a voice says from just outside my door.

It's my dad! But it's too early for the bedbug thing. What's going on?

To tell the truth, I'm still a little mad at him. Why did he believe Mr. Washington at first about me bullying Stanley at school? Yeah, he knows the truth *now*, but he still believed Plaid Dad. And as far as I know, they'd never even met.

I could pretend to be asleep, but like I said before, my dad can always tell when I'm lying. Or faking. Or pretending.

"Mmm?" I answer, trying to sound as sleepy and out-of-it as possible.

Maybe he'll go away.

"May I come in?" Dad says.

"It's your house," I feel like saying, but of course I don't. I am wa-a-a-ay too tired for a lecture on manners.

"Sure," I say instead.

I just hope he doesn't sense with his special Dadly powers that I still have my dirty socks on under the covers, because according to my mom, that's not allowed.

But I was too tired to take them off. Let my feet rot. I don't care.

Dad sits down on the edge of my bed and looks around in the near-dark. Comic books are scattered on the end of my bed, and my sweatshirt, jeans, and belt are crumpled on the floor, right where I left them. There's a half-finished model of a dinosaur on my desk, and a jacket, sweatshirt, and soccer ball are piled on the chair.

Now, Dad probably thinks I'm a slob, on top of everything else bad about me.

"Were you going to say good night?" I ask quickly, before he can criticize me for that, too.

"No," Dad says, his voice low. "I came to offer you an apology, EllRay. I should never have doubted that you were innocent. I know you better than that. I could have at least asked you about it, before jumping to conclusions. So, obviously, even dads make mistakes."

"But how come you *did* believe him?" I mumble from under the sheet I've pulled up to my nose. "You should know a shrimp like me could never bully anyone."

"I know *you* could never bully anyone, son," Dad says, correcting me. "But it's not because you're 'a shrimp,' as you put it. And you'll grow taller, by the way."

I've heard that one before.

"Then how do you know I could never bully anyone?" I ask, my voice a little clearer this time, because I've lowered the sheet.

I kind of bullied Suzette Monahan, didn't I? I don't feel great about that.

"It's not in your character, EllRay," Dad tells me.

My mom is always saying what a character I am, usually after I've done something really goofy, or told her a joke. I love jokes. "You mean because I'm *funny*?" I ask, confused.

"No, son," Dad says. "I mean, because of what you're like inside."

"All bony and icky?" I ask, thinking of this TV crime show I accidentally saw once, over at Kevin's house. Nightmare city. I could barely walk around for a couple of days, knowing all that gunk was inside my body.

I am totally not getting what Dad's trying to tell me.

My dad clears his throat. "Let's see," he says. "Your character is your inner nature, EllRay. Like—you know how sweet and generous your mother is? And loyal, and loving, and creative?"

"Yeah," I say slowly, remembering a second later that my dad likes me to say *yes*, instead.

I am starting to see where this is going.

"That's her character," Dad says, smiling as he looks toward my bedroom door.

He wishes he was with Mom right now. Well, me too!

"What's *your* character?" I ask my dad.

Dad laughs. "I don't think that's for me to say," he tells me. "I hope that at least *part* of my character is that I'm a good father, although I think I could have done a better job of it tonight."

"You're okay," I mumble. "You're good, even. Most of the time. So if this was baseball, you'd be a star! But what about Alfie?" I ask, changing the subject. "What's her character?"

"Too early to tell," Dad says, smiling as he shrugs. "I think she'll blossom into being a proud and lovely young woman some day, though I'd say that being stubborn is always going to be somewhere in the mix. But with any luck, that stubbornness will turn into a willingness to stick with things and work hard. Alfie's already a loving little girl. Look at the way she feels about you, son."

"She *feels* that I wrecked her playdate," I tell him. "And that I made Suzette Monahan not like her. That's how she feels about me."

POW

“Ah, the famous Suzette,” my dad says, his smile disappearing. “There’s always a Suzette around to put a person’s best intentions to the test, isn’t there?”

Does Dad means there will always be dragons to fight? *Always?*

“But Alfie’s crazy about you, son,” Dad adds.

“So,” I say, smoothing my sheet over the blanket like it’s the most important job in the world. “You really think I have a good character?”

“I do,” Dad says, reaching over to rub my head with the flat of his hand, something he likes to do. It’s the mushiest he gets with me. “One of the best. You’re **LOYAL** and **BRAVE**. And forgiving, I hope. But the thing about character is that it isn’t just handed to you when you’re born, and that’s that. You have to keep working on it your whole life long.”

“I’ll have to *work* on it?” I almost yelp.

Like I don’t have *enough* to do? All that homework? And being a good friend to Corey and Kevin? And teaching Alfie stuff, and secretly protecting her from dragons like Suzette Monahan—even if that means dinging up my character a little?

"Hey, don't worry about it, dirty-sock boy," Dad says, adjusting my sheet. "You'll do great. And listen, I'm going to pay for those broken eyeglasses, by the way—except for maybe two allowances from you. Or half of four allowances, so you won't ever be totally broke. How does that sound?"

"Okay," I say, relieved. Because I have a lot of expenses—like candy, comic books, and models of dinosaurs, just to give you a few examples.

"But what about today?" Dad asks, getting back to his apology. "I'm sorry I let you down, son."

"That's all right," I say, leaning against him in the dark. "And sorry about the socks."

"I was just guessing," Dad admits. "So, do you accept my apology?"

"Yeah," I say. "I mean, *yes*. I accept your apology."

"And we're good?"

"We're better than good," I tell my dad. "We're *super*good."

"Then good night, EllRay," Dad says, rubbing my head once more. "And—"

"*Don't let the bedbugs bite!*" we say together.

❊ 18 ❊

COTTON CANDY

"EllRay, pay attention," Mom tells me on Monday afternoon from the front seat of our car—which is still old, but at least has a new battery in it.

Outside our car it is raining a little, but a big storm is on the way, Mom told me this morning. So, as planned, she picked me up from Oak Glen. We are waiting again in the line of cars in front of Kreative Learning and Playtime Day Care. "Sorry. What?" I say, sliding my handheld video game under my backpack, because I know what's coming.

"Dash inside and get Alfie, okay?" Mom says, catching my eye in the rearview mirror.

Grown-ups like to say "dash" when they're talking about *you* running around in the rain, I have noticed. As if you won't get wet if you dash.

"Okay," I say, not bothering to argue. Because the truth is, I'm kind of curious about how things went for Alfie today with her friends Gnarly, Moany, and, most of all, the dreaded Suzette Monahan.

And I'll be able to find out better if I see it with my own eyes.

"What's Alfie wearing today?" I ask, so I can spot her faster. And a **ZING** of sadness goes through my chest as I remember the wadded-up pink jacket under her bed, nestling among the dust bunnies. That jacket was almost brand-new, and it used to be her favorite thing to wear. She said it made her feel like cotton candy.

It's strange how one kid—jealous Suzette, calling it "poop jacket" that day, but wanting it later—could ruin something for Alfie that way. You'd think cotton candy would win out over rabbit poop any day of the week.

But real cotton candy can't stand up to anything, I think, remembering the feeling of a big, cloudy, almost prickly bite of it dissolving into sweetness in my mouth.

It's sweet for just a second, but still.

"I don't remember what Alfie had on this morning when I dropped her off," my distracted Mom says, fiddling with the radio. "Something cute, knowing her. She was asking where her striped sweater was this morning, so maybe she's wearing—"

"That's okay. Never mind," I interrupt as politely as possible, opening the car door. "It's not like I won't recognize my own sister." And I duck my head and dash toward the day care front door.

"Hi, EllRay," the teacher with the clipboard says as I squeeze in past all the excited kids wanting to go home.

"There's my daddy!" one little boy shouts, and the teacher confirms the sighting, checks his name off her list, and watches him scamper—*dash*—to his car.

"Bye, Vlad," the teacher shouts after him, which gives me something to think about as I make my way through the main playroom. Some goofy parents named their kid Vlad? Like the *vampire*? What is wrong with grown-ups?

Maybe "EllRay" and "Alfleta" aren't so bad after all!

I was hoping Alfie and her friends would be jammed into the playhouse in the covered play area, considering the rain. Instead, though, a couple of other girls and a very small boy are playing there. "No, you have to be the *dog*," one of the girls is saying to the boy, who looks like he cut his own hair today with those snub-nosed scissors they make you use in preschool. Boy, is his mom going to be surprised.

I imagine informing those three kids that Suzette Monahan wets her bed.

Naw, they wouldn't care.

I stand under the patio roof and stare out through the raindrops at the yard. Two soggy boys are using the swings, probably trying to remember how to pump. They are flutter-kicking their chunky little legs and bending forward a lot, but they're not getting anywhere. "Push us," one of the boys calls, spotting me.

"Can't," I yell back. "I'm looking for Alfie Jakes."

"She's over *dere*," the other boy says.

He's looking toward the far corner of the yard.

And out from behind the bush near the rabbit hutch come four little girls, their arms linked—but more in an "*I'm not letting go no matter what!*"

kind of way than a "*La-di-dah, we're having so much fun!*" way. There's a big difference.

Suzette leads the line, of course, wearing a navy blue jacket with the hood up. She is followed by Alfie and the other two friends, Moany and Gnarly. Or Gnarly and Moany. I can't tell them apart yet. Maybe it'll be easier once Alfie invites them over to play.

Hey. I'll have to work on that.

But—Alfie's wearing her pink jacket again!

It's wrinkled, and definitely wet, but she's wearing it with confidence. That little jacket seems to glow in the gloomy playground like it's lit up from inside.

Ha! *In your face*, Suzette Monahan.

Alfie's getting there! Her pride is growing—a little, at least.

She *is* a rose.

Suzette twists her skinny body as she runs, whipping her followers around like the tail of a dragon. The little girl on the end—the one with the halo of blonde hair—loses her grip and goes flying off the line.

"Bye, Arletty," Suzette sings out, running hook-armed now with the two other girls in a giant figure eight. It's like she's trying to make them dodge the raindrops.

Arletty scrambles over to the covered patio, laughing. "Hi, Alfie's Brother," she says, looking up at me.

"Hi," I say. "Are you okay?"

"I'm all *wet*," she tells me, sounding surprised as she looks at her arms and legs.

Now, Suzette is running even faster, **ZIG-ZAGGING** like a guy on a football field trying to run the ball closer to the goalpost without getting clobbered.

And—there goes Moany, tumbling off the end of the line. She collapses in a giggling heap, despite the rain.

"Mona," Arletty shouts, holding out her arms. And Mona jumps to her feet and runs to join us.

Now, it's just Alfie and Suzette, out in the rain.

Suzette pauses to stare at Alfie, as if coming up with a new plan to fit this unexpected and unwelcome situation. Then she clamps her linking arm tight, stands in one place, and starts whirling. It's like she and Alfie are on ice skates, they're moving so fast. It's just a pink and navy blue blur. Who is going to let go first?

"*Come on, Alfie. You can do it. Hold on*," I whisper under my breath.

"Al-fie! Al-fie!" Mona and Arletty cheer.

Suzette's navy blue hood flies back as she spins—and then so does she, bouncing once on her rump—like one of Oak Glen Primary School's unofficial dodgeballs. "**OW**," she cries, but she doesn't sound hurt. Not really. You can tell.

Still, Mona and Arletty rush back out into the rain, probably wanting to help Suzette to her feet.

But Alfie gets there first.

She's actually helping Suzette stand up! She's brushing off Suzette's rump!

If that was Jared or Stanley out there, I think, scowling, I'd let them just sit in the rain all afternoon. I'd let them *melt.*

Well, maybe.

I wouldn't brush off their rumps, though. That's for sure.

But Alfie's not me. I guess she gets to decide these things for herself.

"Alfie, *c'mon*," I yell, trying to grab her attention away from the eight-armed hug-fest that seems suddenly to be happening in front of my very own eyeballs. "Mom's waiting in the car!"

"Okay, EllWay," Alfie calls out. And she gives Suzette, Mona, and Arletty a final squeeze, one big enough to last them all until tomorrow. Whatever is going to happen *then.*

My head aches just thinking about it.

And Alfie and her pink jacket rush toward me, as sweet as can be.

Sweet for the moment, anyway.

Like—a mouthful of cotton candy.